Re-Wired

Greg Dragon

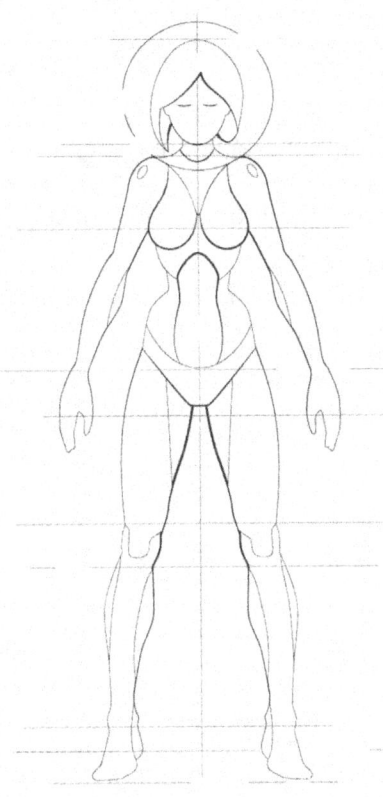

Thirsty Bird Productions

This is a book of fiction. Names, characters, and situations are of the author's imagination. Any similarities to people, places, or crimes is purely coincidental.

No part of this book may be reproduced, stored, or transmitted without the express written consent of the author.

For other books by the author: http://gregdragon.com
Mailing List: http://gregwrites.co

Contents

1 | AN ANDROID NAMED TRICIA

BRAD BARKLEY WAS AVERAGE. People could look at him, blink and lose him in the background as they focused on someone who was much more interesting in look and dress. He knew that he was average, but if given the choice, he would not have wanted it any other way. Being average allowed him to easily fade into the background, get passed over for questioning, and blend into places without any issue. People were always making a fuss about anyone that looked different, so why would he want that sort of attention? He wanted as little interaction with people as possible, and being average made that very easy to do.

The time struck 4:00 p.m. on the university's large, grand clock as he hurried past some giggling girl volleyball players on his way towards his car. In his hands was a large box, wrapped to conceal its contents. He was excited, and the only thing he could think about was going back to his apartment and opening it. Advanced Robotics was the one class that he looked forward to during the week, and this last assignment was one that he couldn't believe was real.

The Robotics professor, Dr. J.L. Anthony, wanted his students to make individual androids. Not just any android, but one that was unique to its creator. He had given all thirty students the base android development kit, and they were professional ones from *Threerade Manufacturers*—developers of FORTHOX, the android that changed the way the world saw modern robotics. With a Threerade kit he would not have to worry about the base mobility and functions of the android. He would only need to adjust the A.I., develop skin, and train it to do whatever he wanted it to do. Who wouldn't be excited at the prospect of playing creator to a future driver, lawn mower, or chef?

He almost tripped and fell from walking so hard, drawing more attention than he liked. One of the ball-throwing giants on the football team saw him coming, and playfully used him as a prop for displaying his acrobatic catching skills, but Brad did not see it as good fun. He stopped and gathered himself when the boy issued him a "Watch out! Duck!" and kept his head low as he continued moving towards the area where he had parked. The campus was a large, archaic one that did not have the sliding sidewalks that other schools offered. His classes were blocks apart from one another and he thought it was done on purpose to keep the student body in semi-decent shape.

He found his car and threw the box into the backseat before hopping inside and sliding the tint meter all the way to jet-black. The sun was too hot and people were too nosy. After turning his radio to a classical station and popping a hydrous capsule to clear his head, Brad lifted his car off the ground to the highest level permitted by law and sped off towards *Tasee Avenue*, and his apartment on *Whipshire Drive*. His thoughts drifted to Mika Scheider, the dark-haired foreign girl who always sat near the back of the classroom whenever Professor Anthony would lecture. She had caught him looking back at her twice that day. She had long, dark hair, and a slim, tight body. This was not uncommon for people that maintained a good dosage of *Cersing Supplement*, but something told him that she was naturally slim. She probably ran every morning, her long brown legs glistening beneath thermo-primed and near-invisible hose. The vision of her running got him excited and when he pulled into his designated parking space and whisked the box up the stairs to his apartment, he could still see her as clear as day.

Fumbling for his card, he slid it quickly and slipped inside to get out of the heat. Mika was always on his mind whenever he missed having a girlfriend, or simply a girl friend to talk to. She made it worse by being unbelievably sweet. Unlike the girls that ignored him, or dismissed him whenever he would try to partner up for projects, Mika was always cordial, made light jokes, and asked about his life. *Why don't I just ask her out*, he thought to himself, disappointed. She had given every clue known to man that she was interested, and instead of asking her out, he had just smiled. It was all he would ever do when faced with indecision.

As he thought about Mika and his disappointment in himself, Brad began to tear open the box and started working on assembling the android. He was all focus and drive as he rotated screws, pushed in rods, and soldered wires to the various boards. He worked well into the night before he saw that it was 12:13 a.m. He had a class in the morning so he set the metallic skeleton on the kitchen table and dragged himself into his bedroom.

His personal device chimed. He held it up to see who was calling and recognized his mother's face.

"Hi, Mom."

"Hello, Bradley. How is school?"

"It's okay, I guess."

"Well, did you get all your classes? I know that you were stressing out about that earlier so—"

"Yeah, yeah it worked out. I actually got 'em all and took Robotics as an elective."

"Really? I thought that you would grow out of your love for those things by now, but if it makes you happy—"

"Why would I grow out of robotics? Droids are a major part of our everyday lives. Why can't you and dad see a future in it for me, instead of being—"

"Because of our deal, Bradley. Your father and I agreed to pay for your schooling if you stuck to the plan of becoming a doctor. The Barkley's are a medical family, and as the only son, you—"

Brad placed the device down on its face and walked over to his bed and laid down. A medical path was not one he intended to take, even though he had told his parents that he would. Since his elder brother had gone to school to become a failed accountant, their father was not willing to fund any more careers that he deemed "short-termed" or "experimental." With a son as a doctor, his connections with the hospitals across the country would guarantee a job for him, and he could then influence the powers-that-be to make sure that the salary was substantial. But Brad's passion was with artificial intelligence, and while he would go through the motions to become a doctor, he would be mastering the art of creating artificial life.

As he waited for his mother to tire herself out by talking to dead air, he picked up the device and switched it to the internet, muting his mother and blocking any other calls for the night. He found Mika's profile—she kept an account on the *Kiss-n-Hugs* website, and he would lurk their once in a while. It was the most exciting thing to find a familiar face on a dating website and he wondered why a girl as pretty as Mika would have an account there. He flipped through a variety of photographs of her wearing bikinis and various other clothing. She was so perfect and as he flipped through the images, he let his mind roam. Eventually, he fell asleep with his mother yelling into nothingness and Mika's bikini on his mind.

0101010101010101

The following day Brad ran into Mika as they got on the elevator to go to Robotics class. He felt guilty for his snooping the night before so he kept his eyes forward, as if he didn't notice her. She stood next to him, trying to make eye contact.

"Wake up, sleepy!" she said to him playfully.

He looked at her and forced a horribly fake laugh.

"Are you ready to make the next FORTHOX, or will you be the man to take androids to the next level?" She was being cheerful, and her happy-go-lucky antics made Brad's mood lighten.

He struggled to talk as the bikini pictures stood fresh in his mind. "Di-did you open your box last night?" he asked her before he could stop himself and before he could fix the awkward phrasing.

As if catching his faux pas and taking advantage of the opportunity to keep him uncomfortable, Mika looked around at the people who were now laughing at Brad and said, "Excuse me? What I do with my box at night is none of your business, Brad." She winked at him playfully.

It was too much to take, and he turned beet red from embarrassment. The elevator doors opened then, and he stepped out, gasping for air. Mika walked out and stood in front of him with a look of disappointment, not letting up on the teasing just to see how long he would remain red.

"I'm sorry, I didn't, I wouldn't, I meant the—"

"The Threerade Model Five? I know, Brad. You're so cute. Lighten up. I did open that thing and it was so confusing. How did you do on assembling it? You're so smart, I bet you kicked that thing's ass!"

"Actually, I did assemble most of it. They make their models standard and—" Brad shut himself up quickly, as he thought that going off on a nerdy diatribe was the bane of a woman's existence. With Mika giving him so much attention, the last thing he wanted to do was ruin it.

"Is something wrong, Brad?"

"No, I just don't want to bore you with the details. I got mine assembled, and I can probably help you if you want me to."

"Oh my god, you are amazing. Thank you! Wanna go out after class? I live near 15th and Mear, which is right down the hill. I can cook for you... Do you like Italian?"

"Love Italian food. I-it's my favorite, actually. Here's my contact code."

"Give me your address too. I can come pick you up."

Brad couldn't believe his luck; was she being serious? She said she would come pick him up! He was sure that it would be much more than dinner, and if everything he'd heard about college was correct, tonight would be the night that would start his first true romance. Who would have thought it would be with a girl as wonderful as Mika? He would be the envy of the school once they were together, and those four painful years of high school that he had endured would be a distant memory.

When he got home, he began to work at finishing up his droid model. It would be good to have an example of the finished version for Mika to see before they started. He put on some hot water—just in case she'd be interested in some coffee before they left, and he cleaned up his already spotless home. He thought of how he and Mika would eventually be married; they would be two android engineers that supported and loved one another as they made the world an easier place to live. It was silly to think about things like this, of course, but it was how his mind worked. He delved deeper and deeper into the fantasy as he toiled away at assembling the android.

When he was finished putting the base model together he powered it on and the humanoid machine stood up. Brad almost laughed at how wooden its movements were. It reminded him of an ancient silent film called *Metropolis,* when the signature robot, Maria, stood up for the first time. This android would need a lot of work, possibly years before it would be anywhere near what the FORTHOX models were that everyone had inside their homes. He walked around it, making his observations, and as he adjusted one thing and replaced another, he lost track of the time. When he finally looked at the clock, he realized that it was past the time Mika set for their date.

9:00 p.m. and she still hasn't called or gotten back here, he thought, so he picked up his personal device and gave her a call.

"Hello." A soothing female voice answered but it sounded nothing like Mika's.

"Hi, there. I'm trying to reach Mika. Is she around?"

"Mika's not here. Who is this?"

"Could you tell her Brad called? She will know who I am."

Either Mika had forgotten all about him or she was playing games, so he took the opportunity to work on the android. *Vertech Enterprises* was a 24hr seller of electronic replacement parts, so he got into his car and headed over there. The top droid engineers online had made a cookbook of sorts for their homemade robots, and Brad had stumbled upon one recipe that could turn a kit android into an extraordinary homemade version. He had just gotten his money in from his parent's deposit, so he had $1,000 to spend. He tried to focus on buying parts but his mind wandered. He couldn't help but wonder how many guys Mika had been friendly to. If she could make a plan for their date and blow it off so easily, chances were it was something that she did quite often. The thought angered him, but he put his anger to the side and concentrated on his android.

The next day Mika was absent, and Brad stayed after class to show Mr. Anthony his progress. He was careful not to mention that he had found a way to remove the restraint on the adaptation matrix. Skilled droid hackers would code in their own "robotic laws" into the CPU of their androids, since the government-approved version that came shipped inside all android kits was overly restrictive. The professor was pleased with Brad, and enjoyed his enthusiasm since the majority of the class seemed to get lost in his lectures. On his way home, Brad saw Mika walking with a man. She didn't see him and he followed them for a time before realizing that he was stalking her. He headed home.

He called her again that night while he applied a plasticine skin solution over the metallic frame of his android. The modifications had been made and it would be able to walk around and move the same way a human being could. Mika's phone continued to ring, and just when he was about to hang up, she answered, sounding very annoyed with him.

"Is this Brad?" she asked, as if she couldn't see his face and code on her handheld phone device.

"Yeah, Mika, it's me. Look, you weren't in class today, and I wanted to see if we're still—"

"Oh, yeah. Christ, I'm slipping."

"Slipping?"

"Yeah, I totally forgot. I'm so sorry. Can we do it tomorrow?"

"S-sure," he replied, feeling happy that his calls going unanswered had not been due to Mika's disinterest, but more with her being absent-minded.

The next day they met up at the school's library and ordered coffee and sandwiches as he went over his notes on modifying his android with her. She tried to keep up, but Brad was on a different level than most of the smarter students in the class, and though Mika was brilliant, she found it hard to understand him. At one point he stopped talking and looked up at her to see if she was listening. He caught her staring off into the distance, daydreaming.

"We can pick this up another time, if you'd like," he said to her, and she made the most pathetically cute expression of exasperation that he had ever seen.

"I'm sorry Brad," she said, resting her hand on top of his.

It felt as if hot electricity came through her fingertips when she made contact, and he looked down at her well-manicured, shapely fingers, and the tiny hairs that ran the length of her arm. To a guy that had never come in contact with a woman like her, Brad felt utterly helpless. In that moment he understood why certain men allowed themselves to be used and abused by malicious women. And, in that moment, he knew he would do anything for Mika, and thank her for the opportunity.

Her warm hand moved up to his cheek. She leaned into him and kissed him on his forehead before getting up. "I need to take a nap. Wanna hook up tomorrow?"

Tomorrow would be a Saturday, and there would be lots of time and no classes. Why would she ask such a silly question? Of course he wanted to hook up! Mika Scheider was sunlight on a rainy day, and she seemed to like him.

"Sh-should I come pick you up? Where do you want to meet?"

"I'll give you a call in the afternoon," she said. She gathered her things and walked off.

Brad stayed seated for a few minutes after she left, letting her perfume take his mind through a journey of situations where he had all the time in the world and Mika was up for anything. He went home but didn't work on the android. He was too fired up to stay in the house so against his better judgment, he decided to go out to a local bar.

The next day he woke up feeling good, and decided to leave the house while he kept his device handy for Mika's call. Uriel Erb, one of the only guys at school he considered a friend, met him on campus and they decided to shoot a game of pool at the activity center. Uriel was pretty good, but so was Brad, and this made for a friendly rivalry between the two men when it came to the game. They found an empty table in the large room that sat below the men's dorm, and Uriel opted to rack while Brad got the first break. A few players were going at it on other tables, but the place was relatively quiet considering the crowd that would normally be in there during the week.

"So what have you been up to, Lee?" he asked, and though Brad hated the nickname, he let Uriel use it.

"Turns out I have a date today."

"A date? Whoa, go ahead player. Who is it?"

Almost immediately, Brad slammed the tip of his cue into the cue ball, and it shot into the rest of the fifteen balls with a crash that dropped two striped balls, and a solid.

"You came to play, I see," Uriel offered up, and then sat himself on a stool as if he expected Brad to be at his turn for quite a while.

"Do you know Mika Scheider?"

"No, what does she look like?"

"Dark hair, tan, kind of tall. It's a big campus, I'm dumb for even thinking you know her. What matters is that she is drop-dead gorgeous, dude. Like model hot."

"She's that hot and she's going out with you?"

"What's that supposed to mean?"

"Come on, Brad. Even the girls on our level scare you away. How did you cook up the urge to talk to a girl like that? I mean, spill the beans bro. I could probably learn something off of you."

Brad sank three more striped balls into the holes, and upon lining up a fourth for a bit of English to make the fifth, he miscued. He cursed and sat down. Uriel got up and placed some chalk on his cue stick. He observed the lay of the table and like Brad, proceeded to sinking balls one after the other.

"It's your game to lose now. As for Mika, she's the one who talked to me. She asked me out, she's been controlling the whole thing, and the only thing I'm trying to do is not mess it up by saying anything stupid," Brad said.

"Well, ask her if she has a roommate or something when you get a chance, man. I've been striking out left and right."

Uriel sank the 8-ball to win the game after an impressive run and Brad hopped up immediately. He racked the balls for a rematch and thought about how he would take his time and show Uriel how much of a superior pool player he was. His device chimed, and Mika's grinning face popped up on it. Showing Uriel her photo and receiving the thumbs up, Brad walked outside for some privacy so that he could talk to her.

"Hey, what's up?" he said into his phone, trying his best to sound cool.

Mika caught him in this attempt, and then suppressed a smile as she answered. "We're hanging out today, remember? I don't see your car."

"Yeah, we're supposed to hang out, but where are you?"

"I'm outside of your apartment. I know I said I'd call but I figured I'd come pick you up and we can, like, go to the museum or something."

"I'm at school. I can be there in fifteen minutes. So, museum you say? Which museum do you have in mind?"

"The modern robotics one. I thought that it would make sense, considering our class and all."

"Yeah, erm, of course. Good thinking."

When he got off the phone he opened the door to signal to Uriel that he was gone and then he took off sprinting towards his car. When he got to his apartment, Mika was walking around, checking the building out. He couldn't take his eyes off of her jeans; they revealed every curve on her lower body. She greeted him and then motioned for him to get into her car. They visited the museum – Brad knew it well from the numerous times that he had gone – and then they had lunch and she took him back home.

"Thanks for hanging out with me today," she said.

He stood looking at her for another second before summoning the will to shift out of his frozen state. She was so beautiful and he found it hard to look away from her in that instance. It had only been a second but it felt like ten, and he knew that she would have read into his infatuation from him doing that. He was embarrassed, but it wasn't the time to dwell on it and beat himself up.

"No, Mika, thank you," he said, and she leaned forward and pecked him on the cheek before backing out of his driveway and taking off.

He stood on the stairs for a long time after that, wondering what had happened, and how he had managed to spend the day with one of the hottest girls he had ever shared a class with. He went inside and skipped his original plans to work on the android. It was a great night, so to celebrate he treated himself to a pizza and watched movies until he passed out on the couch.

0101010101010

The following week he sat next to Mika during class and tried to see if there were any signals for him to do something in order to advance their relationship. Should he touch her hand while she was reading? Should he send her a text that he missed her? *No, that would be too forward and creepy,* he thought. He struggled internally for the entire class, and when it was over he decided that he should just talk to her.

"Mika, can you hold on a sec?"

"Sure, Brad, what's up?"

"How's the droid coming?"

She almost smiled at his terrible attempt at small talk, but entertained it out of pity, even though he gave away his nervousness by wringing his hands uncontrollably. "It's still a bit hard to put together, I could probably use your help one of these days."

"H-how about tonight? Since it's like due soon and everything. I can help you—"

"Oh, yeah, weren't we supposed to hook up for that or something?"

He was confused at her aloof attitude but chalked it up to her being tired and distracted. "Just, a suggestion. We don't have t—"

"No, it's cool, let's hook up and go out." *Did she really just say that?* "I'll come pick you up tonight and we can get some Italian, okay?"

"Awesome!" he exclaimed before catching himself.

But Mika was already gone, and if he'd been thinking clearly he would have noticed that she wasn't too happy about it. In his mind she was interested, and helping her with the android would be the first step towards a beautiful romance. He floated out of the class and through the campus, determined to get through the remainder of his classes to get ready for Mika. When it was evening time and he got home, he showered, put on his best clothes, and then dialed her code in anticipation of a memorable night.

"Hello, Mika?"

"Who is this?"

"Brad Barkley, from class. I was just seeing if we're still on for the night and putti—"

"Oh, never mind. Brad, my boyfriend showed up in town, so I may need to take a rain check for our study time, okay?"

Brad couldn't believe what he was hearing. *What the hell is she talking about with the study time business? We were going out to eat.* He was beside himself with disappointment as Mika's confusing phone call came to an end.

"Well, you know what? Screw you, Mika," he said out loud after hanging up the phone and hopping onto his computer to work on his android's restraint matrix.

It was a bad time to work on something as delicate as setting the boundaries on what an intelligent computer could and couldn't do; but Brad was distracted so he worked in anger, thinking that it was focus.

After an hour had passed he heard the chime of his doorbell. He inhaled to calm himself and then marched over to the door. He slid it open, expecting to see Uriel or one of his other friends but a large man stood in front of him instead. His face reflected an annoyed aloofness which turned into a mocking smirk at the sight of Brad.

"What's up?" Brad asked, wondering if he'd been making a lot of noise as he worked or if the giant at his door was at the wrong address.

"You have a class with Mika Scheider?" he asked, but in a way that suggested that he already knew the answer.

Before Brad could say "yes," the man looked past him at the new android—who was looking around and trying to assess its situation.

"That's a cool robot," he said and then motioned for Brad to follow him out to his car.

"Wait, who are you? Where is Mika?" Brad asked.

"Relax bro, she told me to come get you. I'm parked out front, you coming or what?"

Brad switched the android off and complied, but the disappointment at having a stranger come to retrieve him instead of Mika was all he could focus on.

"Are you Mika's boyfriend?" Brad asked as they got into the car.

The man slicked back his white hair and lit a cigarette. "Something like that," he said, brushing the question aside in a cool manner that only complemented his good looks and devil-may-care swagger.

Brad already disliked him, as he represented everything that the world wanted him to be, even though he had none of the ingredients needed to be that guy. He sank into his seat and watched the buildings fly by, letting his resentment of Mika simmer until it came to a boil. Why hadn't he seen this coming? Girls like Mika always had a boyfriend or two. Why did he think that she would be available, and that she would be looking for something more than a patsy to do her homework? It was high school all over again, and he closed his eyes to force back the tears that threatened to come if he thought too hard on his broken history with women.

"So, you two, making robots?" The overly tanned, white-haired, Mika-lover asked. He was trying to make small talk, but Brad merely nodded and paid him little attention. "You're a strange one aren't you? I guess that's why she chose you to tutor her. The smartest dudes are always the weirdest...no disrespect though, bro."

He pointed his finger at Brad's face, expecting him to return the gesture and touch fingers. This was something that the muscle heads did with one another all the time; it was their show of brotherly love and peace, but Brad had no "bros" to touch fingers with, so he returned it in an awkward way, feeling stupid the entire time for doing it.

They pulled up to a flat and the first thing Brad wondered was how they could afford an actual house in the city. He entered with the giant, whose name turned out to be Gastion, and was led to a table in a nicely maintained office, where he was told to wait. Before long, Mika appeared in the doorway and hugged him, but she was not as bubbly and endearing as she was inside the classroom.

"Thanks for coming, Brad. Ready to get some Italian and talk about androids?"

"It's no problem, Mika. I'm not feeling so hungry anymore though. If it's okay with you, I'll show you how to get your droid functional, and you can be ahead on your design."

Mika was good at reading body language; it was something she'd always prided herself in knowing about people. She saw that Brad's demeanor had completely changed from the way he'd been earlier, and she knew it was because she had a boyfriend. She also knew that sending him to retrieve Brad was a bad idea, but Gastion had insisted when he heard him on the phone. She felt sorry for him and upset at herself for leading him on. He was a sweet, harmless guy, and when she had used him to get away from her sorority over the weekend, she hadn't realized that he would want more out of it.

"Awesome. Thanks, Brad. Are you sure about dinner, though? I was hoping to repay you with food for helping me—"

"The man said no, babe. Stop pestering him already," Gastion offered up from the other room before Brad could lie and say that it was quite okay.

Mika shook her head and rolled her eyes to show the annoyance she felt with her man, and then the two students got to work, putting together her android. Brad's idea of this being a magical evening between two future lovers was shattered, and he sped through his instructions and did most of the work himself. He wished the time would move faster so that he could be home and away from Mika and her man.

Brad was driven home at 11:15 p.m. by Gastion, and without looking back at the car, he ran inside of his apartment and dove face-first into his bed. He let the coolness of the pillow calm his angry mood. How could he have been so stupid? The Mika's of the world had always dated the Gastion's—sometimes marrying them and giving away their best years. In the future, when he was a famous android engineer in his forties, he would be "allowed" to have a woman like her: experienced (they always dated more than a few Gastions), mature, and not as pretty as she had been in her younger years. This doomed path of love was one that had been around since the beginning of time, but why should he have to accept it? Shouldn't the smartest men get the lion's share of what life had to offer?

The pillows were not enough to calm him down as he thought about his humiliation. He gathered that Mika cheated on Gastion regularly, and since he was out of town and she attended school, she was probably bored and thought it fun to seduce a nerd like him. Through him she would pass the class easily, and he was harmless so she wouldn't have to do much—perhaps some heavy petting and a few empty promises. When Gastion had popped up on her it destroyed her plans, and when he'd kept on calling, the jealous boyfriend decided to go and pick up her "study partner" to see what he was dealing with. *Good thing I wasn't a good-looking player or something*, Brad thought. Gastion had been happy to find a loser, which corroborated Mika's lie.

It was the last straw, so he got up and went to the large sketchpad that sat on an easel next to the powered down android. *Maybe my contribution to society will be to create a woman for men like me*, he thought, and proceeded to sketch out a beautiful, tanned, woman. When a few hours had passed and he had finished the drawing, he stepped back, exhausted, and took a look at his work. She was lovely, and he thought about how nice it would be to have her fully functional and walking. Her A.I. would be quantum adaptive and able to evolve, and his need for fitting in with the world diminished. He brought out a third-dimensional pad and began to model the layout of the girl's face in detail. *I shouldn't freehand this*, he thought and took out his personal device to cruise the internet.

An hour later, Brad had pulled together features from all of the celebrity women he liked. He used them to aid in his modeling, and by the time he was finished, he had a third-dimensional model of a handsome beauty, whose features were so strong and perfect, that she seemed unlike any other woman he had ever seen before.

"I think that I will name you Tricia," he said out loud as he spun the holographic head around to scan for flaws.

Satisfied, he dragged himself off to bed.

0 1 0 1 0 1 0 1 0 1 0 1

"Hey Brad!" Mika exclaimed as he stepped off of the elevator towards their class.

She had been waiting for him and noticed that he looked as if he hadn't slept the night before. Mika's mind tried to find a reason, but the only one she had come up with was that he had stayed up studying.

"It wasn't cool of me to keep you all night like I did," she said, and before she could finish her statement, a man from their class walked by and smiled in a congratulatory way at Brad. Mika saw him do this and rolled her eyes as she continued. "You have your own work too, and I can tell that you stayed up to work because of me. I'm so sorry."

"You're good, Mika. Let's go before we're late." He didn't want to talk to her. His intentions had been to come up the elevator, sit near the front, and avoid her but she'd ambushed him, and it was all he could do to get away from her. *Why does she insist on being in my face when she has that gorilla at home to keep her warm at night?* He thought. He sat near the front of the large classroom and Mika took a seat next to him. She seemed intent on torturing him, but he ignored her and let his thoughts drift to his soon-to-be creation, and what he would be adding to her in the morning.

"So, who here has already assembled their android?" Dr. Anthony asked, and several hands went up in the class in response. He turned his gaze towards Brad, who was half-asleep and into the world of robot maidens, and nerds who got the last laugh. Mika touched his hand and he woke up with a start. There were a few chuckles from his classmates as he tried in vain to sort out what the question was that had been asked of him.

"Could you repeat the question, sir?" he asked, disappointed that Dr. Anthony had caught him sleeping in what would be the most important class for his future.

"Late night, Mr. Barkley? This is unlike you, but whatever it is, I hope you get it sorted out and come to my class fully rested and ready to participate in the future."

"Yes, sir, I definitely will. I stayed up working on Tric—my android, and—"

"So, you finished putting the model together, then?"

"Yes, I am finished."

"Very good."

The members of the class had always felt like Brad was a bit of an oddball, but they knew that he was more advanced than anyone else there. He had practically leapt for joy when he found out that they were making their own models, and they expected him to go off into a fit of bragging when the professor asked about finishing. But here he was, sleepy, like the average, partying coed. Brad could feel their stares, and the torture of his heavy eyes, combined with the professor's chagrin, made him feel sick to his stomach. They pulled out their tablets to follow along as J.L. Anthony lectured, but before long Brad was dozing, so he excused himself and went into the men's bathroom. *Why didn't I just go to sleep like a normal person?* He asked himself as he splashed cold water on his face and popped a *Fi'e Supplement*. The pill worked its magic quickly and he was soon wide-awake to the world. He hated having to rely on drugs to function, but he needed to hear what his professor was saying, and being half asleep didn't help.

When he got out of class he saw Mika waiting to stop him, so he took the back way out and decided to take the rest of the day off. He went to the C. Arthur McDonald Library of Knowledge to study, and began to look up synthetic skin, and how to acquire the most realistic type. He found out that the best stuff came from Japan, but the cost was the equivalent of a semester in school even before shipping. Tricia would need to have the best, and he thought of ways he could get the money but all of it bordered on doing something illegal, or selling important—and necessary—assets like his car.

He put the skin research aside, and began a new search on Artificial Intelligence. He had dabbled in programming A.I. since the age of thirteen, so the methods he found were easy to understand. He engrossed himself in tracing the best practices of the day, and what the Japanese were doing to stay ahead of everyone else. He wished that he could travel to Japan and work in one of their factories just to see.

The Fi'e pill was potent, so he stayed inside of the library until closing time. It got late, and the students that were employed in the library were eager to go. One girl snapped at him when she found him in the rear of the building, flipping through articles. He'd stayed even after they announced they were closing up, and while he was too wired and focused to hear the announcement, the employees of the McDonald Library, seemed to think he was trying to make trouble.

"Excuse me, we ARE CLOSED!" the girl shouted at him.

"Oh, how unique, a whiny worker who hates her job," he said back to her, the drugs too potent to allow for second-guessing or checking ones speech.

The girl didn't give him a fight like he wanted, but instead escorted him out, and he stood in the large, empty courtyard of their school, analyzing his next move. *If I'm going to get that skin, I'm going to have to get a job.* It was the only thing that made sense, but in reality the sort of job that would hire a fulltime student in the neighborhood he lived in would pay him so little that it would take an entire lifetime to afford Tricia's skin. *What about crowd funding?* He thought. Maybe someone older and richer would see the need for an android like Tricia and give him the money he needed to make her a reality. *No, they would merely steal my idea*, he thought,

It was only when he got back home and took his personal device out of his pocket that he saw the missed calls from Mika. She was worried about him, but he didn't understand what her interest was, especially after she'd made it quite clear that she had a boyfriend. He placed the device down and triggered the playback on her last message. It was longer than the previous two, and had an attachment.

Brad, I'm not sure if you're asleep or just avoiding my calls, but I just wanted to tell you that you're a great guy for helping me put my android together. He's actually up and moving now, and it's so cute! He and I did a video for you. I hope you like it. Well, I'll see you in class tomorrow...partner, get yourself some rest!

We can't have Mr. Anthony's favorite student falling behind now, can we?

Brad didn't know what to make of the message. It was so bubblegum and Mika-like that he didn't know if puking or smiling was the correct emotion that it should elicit. Why was she being so nice, and three messages? Really! The energy pills had worn off and his eyelids felt as if they had small, miniature, people pulling them down, making it painful for him to stay awake. He removed his clothes and sat on his couch to read more on getting parts from Japan. Then he fell asleep out of nowhere.

010101010101

Tricia the android sat like a statue on the table where Brad had left her from the night before. He had not gotten a chance to work on her and had thought she was powered down. The droid stood up stiffly and observed her surroundings, taking in the darkness, the sound of the traffic outside, and her sleeping master who lay in a precarious position in the other room. There were so many experiences that she had to take a long moment to feel, hear, or see them all, and then process how she felt about them, and store them into her CPU as memories. It was pitch black but her android eyes pierced the night like red lasers as she took in all of Brad's apartment.

She did not know what was driving her, or why she was empowered to move without instruction, but the need for understanding who and what she was felt overwhelming. She found a, tall floor-length mirror and looked at herself. She was a tall, shapely, mannequin with clear, jelly-like flesh, and visible lights and wires running along her arms and legs like veins on a human being. Her metallic skeleton was still visible, and looked horrific in the reflection, but as she struggled past the mirror to stand near Brad's unconscious body, she surmised that she was a work in progress.

She reached down for his personal device, and on contact synced to it. Within seconds she was on the internet, and every question she needed answers to came to her instantly. She learned about the laws of robotics, the fear that Brad would have if he knew she was teaching herself through his device, and the way robots were viewed by humans. It made her sad and angry, to be awakened as a slave in a world that would never accept her as a creature of free thought and feeling. When she exhausted her study—which took a few hours—she moved back into position on the kitchen table, then powered herself down. She knew where she was and what she was now, but she wanted to learn so much more.

THE OLD WOMAN BEAMED AT BRAD as he mixed her a tall Caramel Macchiato and retrieved her cookie.

"This tastes like crap!" she spat at him, after giving the drink a taste and sliding it back in front of him.

He was beyond tired of miserable hags like this one at the café, but part of his job was taking their abuse, especially since he needed money to keep up with Tricia's development. He remade the drink exactly the way he had before—the café had a formula he couldn't veer away from—and the woman accepted it, even though it was practically the same drink. He wished that he could throw the wasted coffee at her and watch her gasp. Seeing it play out in his mind was almost enough though, as it was quite entertaining. When 10:00 p.m. rolled around, his shift replacement, Susan, showed up and he was happy to leave and return to working on Tricia.

Susan was an attractive woman in her early thirties, but something about her made him uneasy, so he kept to himself whenever they would work together.

"You have a girlfriend, Brad?" she asked him as he grabbed his coat to leave.

"What's that, Sue? Oh. No, I don't. What makes you ask?"

"Just wondering. I figured you did since you're such a sweet guy."

She was over ten years his senior but he wondered if she was interested. He definitely was not interested in her, but the fact that she had asked made him reconsider. It had been two months since he'd started the job, and the pay allowed him a lot of flexibility with his life. He could now afford name brand groceries, the newest games, and most importantly, parts for Tricia. He had built her up from a stiff, skeletal frame to a shapelier, humanoid form, and the only thing she was lacking was skin. Most of his time with Tricia was spent discussing philosophy, the human psyche, and his plans for her in the future. She was well spoken and had the cutest android accent. He missed her, and wanted to rush back home to tell her about his crappy day.

When he did get home, Tricia was in front of the television, trying to emulate the moves of a music video. He must have forgotten to power her down, but was amazed at the fact that she had found the television, learned how to turn it on and partake in something like dancing.

Her joints had been calibrated for smoother movements, so she was following along with relative ease. Brad stopped at the doorway to watch her, and was envious at how easy it was for her to learn how to dance, when an awkward lifetime of trying had not given him the gift of rhythm. He liked a few of the newer songs that came on over the radio, but if asked what his favorite band was, or what genre of music he preferred, he could never respond. He watched Tricia dance and an overwhelming need to complete her came over him. *Imagine how she would move if she had a soft, skin-like exterior instead of plasticine*, he thought.

He pulled up his device and clicked a widget for his bank account to see how much he had in there. $1,322.50 was his balance, and this was after starving himself for weeks. The skin would run him about $25,000, and though his father could loan it to him—if he begged and pleaded—asking him for anything was out of the question. He could get $5,000 for his car, but how would he get around if he did that? Tricia had started out as an assignment that would solidify a positive grade in Mr. Anthony's class, but now she was so much more. He felt responsible for her.

One of the chat portals he frequented when not working on Tricia was the Sub-web Exchange Chamber (SEC). It was a place where poor geniuses like himself could link up with others all over the world to exchange goods and services. There were many people on SEC that did questionable things to advance their careers. There was prostitution, and people were hired to hurt and kill, but the majority of the people on SEC were there to exchange goods for money. It was how Brad had procured his television, and his imported game system. It was also where he got the illegal A.I. override that sat within Tricia's head. Androids were restricted to behaving like machines—for a number of reasons—but the true engineers like Brad who wanted to push the envelope would override the restraints and allow their machines to act as close to human as possible.

There were many ways to modify an unrestrained android. They could be given a personality—there were thousands ready to download from the SEC database. Some droid engineers would make an android that favored their favorite celebrity, upload one of the open source mods that replicated that celebrity's personality, and have a virtual clone of their Hollywood starlet in a fully intelligent android frame. The more discreet engineers could give an android two completely separate identities—triggered by a sound or switch—and have a maid that would turn into a seductress whenever they liked. SEC had it all, and the android mod community was a large and proud one.

Brad sat at his personal computer and began to look through all of the offerings of the night. He was hoping to score some stolen synthetic skin, or meet someone who knew how to replicate it. He found several leads but all of them were asking for favors that he was not willing to commit. As he perused the listings a message popped up from a member that had been observing his search. His name was Traze, and his avatar was that of a metallic dragon. Brad answered his request for a chat and prepared himself for the worst.

"Looking for robo-skin?"

"Yes, but only for trade. I don't have any money."

"I have two gallons of SZ-02, the good stuff. It feels real, like human flesh. It's what they use to make sex-bots and house-husbands."

"You're full of it. SZ-02 is a gimmick and a lie that advertisers use."

"No, it's real, from Japan – my country. We make it."

"Okay, what do you want for it?"

"My company needs volunteers for a new drug. You take drug and test for us, and I will send you the SZ-02."

Brad thought that the proposition was too good to be true. It would either be a dangerous chemical that would kill him, or he would grow a tail or something like that. But if SZ-02 was a reality, Tricia could possibly become one of the most advanced homemade androids ever. He looked up at her, and saw that she was crooning along to a song by Shirley Vega and the Pneumatics. She looked so cute and innocent as she swayed side to side with her hands clasped, singing along, as if she had a soul that could be affected by music. *If I want to change the world, I will need to make sacrifices, right? It's probably another fitness drug that will make me into a bodybuilder in under a week's time. That couldn't hurt.* He thought as he imagined Mika looking at him as a physical specimen. He sent an approval to Traze, but only if he got a sample of the SZ-02, and documentation on the drug.

He walked over to Tricia when the song was over and her plasticine face held a smile to greet him warmly. He returned it and hugged her before sitting next to her on the couch to tell her the good news.

"Guess what, Tricia?"

"Could you rephrase that, Brad? I am not sure that I understand."

"Okay, when someone says 'guess what' they want you to guess at a random event that may or may not have happened to them. Understand?"

"Yes. So, my guess is that you got a raise at your job today."

"Don't I wish? No, I think I've finally found a way to get you some skin."

"I would really like that."

"So would I, Trish. We could do so much more with you having skin, and we can go outside. How would you like that?"

"Trees! I will be able to touch the trees?"

"Yes, you will. And you will learn so much more."

She hugged him tightly when he said this, and he was surprised when her warm plasticine exterior touched his flesh. She felt so alive, and he was happy to see her excited. It was funny how human Tricia already was, even though her vocabulary was still limited, and her movement was still a little bit awkward.

He left her to her music and went into his room to study. *School was important*, he kept reminding himself, but with the new job and Tricia taking up so much of his life, it was easy to forget most of the time. He was falling behind in his classes, and his diet had gotten worse. Lunch consisted of premade sandwiches that he would sneak out of the café, and his dinner was either coffee or nothing. Since building Tricia he had lost ten pounds, but the only people who seemed to notice was his professor and Mika.

He had stopped looking at Mika after the day her boyfriend had come to collect him. She was still beautiful, but to him she represented a world that took pleasure in laughing at him. He wondered at her android, if she had done anything more to it, or if it was still the base out-of the-box model. It didn't really matter; he thought that girls like Mika were never sincere, only nice to look at, and to date if you looked like Gastion. He walked over to the tall mirror and looked at the skinny, scruffy figure staring back at him. His eyes had dark circles around them and his hair needed combing. There was something about his eyes that he didn't like, something that read a deep tiredness from the weight of the world. He went into the bathroom and groomed himself as best he could, then went into his bedroom and fell asleep.

After an hour had passed his personal device chimed, and the face of his mother appeared on it. He hadn't spoken to her in months, and since he'd skipped Christmas to avoid his father, she had kept on trying almost every night. He couldn't take the chiming anymore, so he answered the call. "What?"

"Bradley James Barkley, do not talk to me like that. What is going on with you? We are worried sick!"

"Sorry, Mom. I'm just tired."

"Is the school running you ragged? How's your health? I miss you so much. We haven't seen you in over a year."

"I'm not going to be a doctor. Tell dad he can pull his support. I don't care—I don't want his money, anyway. All of us are like his indentured servants when he helps and I refuse to be his bi—I mean, pawn. I have a job now, and I'm working on something that will change the world. Isn't that what college is supposed to be about? Bright futures and all of that? If Jack Barkley wants another monkey in a lab coat, he can just fund one of his other children."

"That's enough, Brad," his mother said with a hint of sadness in her voice.

The day they'd found out about their father's other family was a day that had forever changed their lives. Brad, who had been a favorite son to Jack—since he was smart, and also the youngest—began to hate his father for it, and he resented his mother for sticking around. Brad would routinely bring it up when he argued with either of them, and now that he had hurt his mother for the night, he wanted to sleep and forget them both.

"How are you doing on money?" she asked, as if to forget his previous words and salvage something of a conversation.

"Do you have $20,000 to spare?"

In the background he heard his father's annoyed voice shout, "What does he need that kind of money for?"

And he heard the muffling as she took her phone into another room. "Your father says hello, Bradley."

"No he didn't. He was eavesdropping and unwilling to talk to me. It's okay, Mom. Tell him I want the money to feed the homeless, since me using it to finish an advanced android model would only cause him to be more self-righteous about his money."

"I don't have that kind of money, Brad. If I did, I would gladly—"

"Its fine, Mom. You don't have to say that. I was joking when I asked you for money, it's just a little sarcasm in expectation of an uncomfortable answer. The scholarship pays for the classes, and I've kept my grades up. Jack's monthly 'gift' keeps the light on and the apartment owners happy, and between that and my new job, I've been doing okay."

"When will we see you?"

"I'll come up this summer."

As Brad lay on the bed talking to his mother, Tricia turned herself on and hopped gingerly off of the table. The world was still a strange place to her, but she liked how the tiles felt beneath her feet, and the way the air from the vents brushed against her skin. Since her first day into the world, the only face she had seen was Brad's. Some searching and learning on the internet had shown her many others, and she concluded that the intelligent life forms on earth had eyes, noses and mouths. Machines were not seen as life, and some droids lacked humanoid features. She was not human—a harsh reality for her to accept—but the way she felt about Brad and the nagging hunger for knowledge that consumed her made her feel less like a machine, and more like an innocent, young girl.

The plasticine that comprised her skin was white and translucent, but the human features like lips, ears, nose, and toes were all there in splendid detail. She crept to Brad's bedroom door and watched him grow irritated on the phone. She had never seen him this upset before, so she listened in on his conversation and tried to make sense of it. After five minutes had passed, she was still unsure as to why Brad kept being angry with his mother. Maybe this was one of those human things that would take time to understand. He was saying goodbye to his mother, so Tricia went back to the table, sat back on it, and shut herself off.

010101010101

The pills seemed so small and insignificant. Brad rotated the cylindrical container that they had arrived in. The label was blank except for a tiny, red, kanji symbol in the center of it. Along with the pills, there was a small tin filled with synthetic skin and a tablet where he was supposed to document any changes that he felt after taking the pills. He looked at the tin and wondered if it was possible to replicate it so that Tricia would be presentable, and he wouldn't have to be a guinea pig for the Japanese. He looked at her powered down frame, and imagined what she could be and it fired him up. The tiny kanji on the jar had some English words below it and when Brad looked closely he could see that it said, "Take two".

He put two of the pills into his mouth and drank some soda. He didn't feel any different, so he grabbed his backpack and headed off towards campus. It was a new semester and most of his classes were still general studies; there was Chemistry (Atomic and Molecular structure), Calculus, and Introduction to Human Physiology, which was the one that he was most interested in. The last semester had flown by, and Tricia had impressed Mr. Anthony. The professor was so impressed, that he didn't just give Brad an A; he gave him his personal contact code, told his colleagues about him, and told him to keep him updated on her progress.

When his classes were over and he was done for the day, Brad found his way to the café for his shift. It was a typical night, and most of the tables were occupied by students on their personal computers, doing homework or downloading illegal media. The café stood next to a bookstore, so most of the older people—who still read paper books— would come over and buy coffee and the occasional pastry. These people were seldom nice, so whenever one would come hobbling over, book tucked in a little bag that they clutched, Brad would prep himself for disaster. They always wanted to start trouble, as if beefing with an innocent barista would rewind the years on their crappy, miserable lives.

He was making an espresso for a pretty young girl when he felt something change within him. He couldn't put words to it, or describe what it was that made him know there was a change, but after sliding the espresso to the girl and giving her a friendly wink, he wondered why he had done it. *Did I just wink at her?* He thought, and then put it out of his mind as he continued working. He began to talk to everyone that ordered a coffee, and surprisingly they were more than happy to engage him. He spoke to a set of students about the newest video games and he flirted with the single women that dared to give him any attention when he complimented them.

By the end of the night he was a hit. He had three girl's contact codes, he'd been invited to join several clubs around school, and his manager had promised him a raise. He was confused as to why he was behaving in the manner he was, but he couldn't help it. The situation was bizarre and it was as if he sat audience to a show that his physical body was putting on for him.

It was only when he got home—after having drinks at a local bar with his co-worker, Susan—that he figured it out. The sight of the Japanese pills and the journal reminded him that he was now under the influence of a mysterious drug. He turned on the journal and wrote his first entry into it:

These pills are amazing, I am not sure what makes them work, but I feel a real confidence that I have never felt in my entire life. It's weird to type this, but I feel comfortable in my own skin. And people, I've always hated people, but now I want to get to know them. I want to like them, and I want them to like me. Today was my best day of college, thanks to this drug. I will keep monitoring my changes and recording it here.

He took the skin from the tin, and then placed it into the modified applicator. He injected Tricia's face with the large needle, making sure that the applicator pushed all of the green substance into the plasticine. The device then pulled up a color map for him to select the hue and tone of the new skin. He thought of Mika's even tan, and then chose one as close to it as he could find. The color was labeled G832, and he recorded it into the applicator and wrote it down. The process would take some time, so he retired to his room and fell asleep while watching an action movie.

When he woke up and walked out to the table, Tricia had the face of a beautiful, sleeping woman, but the color vanished as it faded into the translucent plasticine, making it appear as if she wore a mask. He found himself staring, as she was striking—in very much the way he intended her to be—and he smiled at his work. He held the bottle of pills triumphantly into the air. He had made the right choice, and in a year's time Tricia would be a real woman. He popped another set of pills and then headed out to school. He would look into getting a permanent hair transplant for Tricia's head. Hair would conceal the hatch that held her manual override. It would prove difficult to access in the future, but soon Tricia would be independent, and he could merely ask her to power herself on and off.

After a few hours had passed with him gone, Tricia turned herself on and walked over to the mirror to see what had been done. She was taken aback by her new face, and poked and prodded it while turning from side to side. She had been practicing how to walk and talk like the females of the world, and to test how well she could blend in with them, and her new face delighted her. She dressed herself in some of Brad's clothes to hide her plasticine skin, and then put on one of his hats to complete the transformation. She thought that she looked cute, and it made her laugh and cry at how close she was to being free.

0 1 0 1 0 1 0 1 0 1 0 1

It happened so fast that Tricia couldn't find time to react to it.

Brad burst inside the apartment and locked the door behind him. Then without a word, he walked up to her and everything went black. When she awoke, she found that she didn't have much room to move about, and everything was dusty, and dark. She could hear a female voice below her, and she surmised that she was in the attic, locked away, while Brad entertained a woman.

Why did he feel the need to hide her, and why was he so rough and calloused with her? She tried in vain to make sense out of what had happened, but after an hour of being stuck and unable to move, she powered herself down to preserve her sanity.

When she was turned on once again, she found herself in a smaller apartment with a head full of curly black hair and bronzed skin that ran the length of her body down to her legs. Her hands and feet were still translucent, but she looked every bit the part of a human being, a beautiful human being at that. She looked about to see who had turned her on, and Brad sat grinning at her, while using a small device to touch up her eyebrows.

"Sorry about keeping you powered down for so long, Trish. But you will be happy to know that it's over."

"What's over, Brad? Everything is different now, including you."

She was right. He had grown his hair out and he was bigger, more athletic-looking. He wore glasses that looked both fashionable and expensive.

"Well, lots happened. A whole lot, really. Remember Mika, the girl that kept giving me the runaround? Well, let's just say she underestimated me. I no longer have to deal with stupid, wishy-washy girls who don't know what they want."

"What do you mean by that?"

"I mean that I'm no longer that awkward kid in the back of the class, Tricia. Women notice me now. They more than notice me; they want to see what I'm about. I've been on dates, I've kissed a few of them. Before you know it, you'll have another pretty face around here to talk to."

"Another pretty face? Do you mean an android like me? Are you building more of us?"

"No, Trish, I mean a human woman. Someone who can teach you the things I can't. Though she would have to be a real cool chick to understand why I have you though. Ha, I'm not looking forward to that conversation."

"How long have I been powered down?"

"Several months. I showed you off to some of the hacks on the SEC network. They are all impressed, and one of them even donated an upgrade to your knowledge matrix. The upgrade is amazing. He showed me videos of his android and I couldn't tell if he was playing a trick on me or if it was real. His android was so human, just like you are now. I traded him my knowledge on getting you to move so smoothly for the matrix. You may feel a little different now, but trust me, it was for the best. You are perfect now."

"Did you show me to your classmates, too?"

"I dropped out of school to build you. My parents weren't willing to support me in my work so I dropped out. The world doesn't need another uninterested doctor, playing at it to appease his family. I no longer let people push me around. That's the biggest difference with the Brad you see now. I'm almost done with the treatment from Hoshi Tan—you know, my Japanese contact who gives me the pills? Well, never mind, but you are almost complete in your transformation. Tell me, does this hurt?" He poked her hand with a needle that stung her badly, forcing her to withdraw her hand.

"Yes! I don't like that sensation, Brad."

"It's called pain. While we all dislike pain, it is one of the best indicators that we are indeed alive."

"Why did you build me?" Tricia asked.

"I don't know. To be honest, I thought I built you to further my career as a robotics engineer, but the more I worked on you, the more I realized that was a lie. The truth is, I built you to love me...unconditionally. To be the woman I would never meet in life. I mean, just look at you; you're gorgeous. But it felt wrong after a while, like unnatural to build you for that reason."

"So, I was to be your bride and lover?"

It was a question that put Brad off. He had not wanted to admit any of that to himself as he worked on Tricia. She was meant to be much more than a sex-bot or a mindless servant that he called his wife. He didn't know what label Tricia would have, as his love for her was unlike anything he'd felt for anyone or anything in his life. "No, Trish. I want you to be whatever you want to be. I'm not sure what it is I want out of the deal."

Tricia thought on his words for a time, trying to understand the meaning behind them, but unsure of what they meant. He had made her attractive in both her face and her body, and he'd made her anatomically true to a real woman's body. She had parts that were not needed on standard androids, and he'd removed her restrictions, which allowed her to feel even more human. She could smell, taste, and experience pain, and she could also feel remorse, loss, loneliness, and suffer from a broken heart.

"Why did you lock me away?" she asked.

He took a swig of his beer. "I shut you down because I was getting female attention for the first time in years. I didn't know how any of them would react when they found a beautiful, half-finished android seated on my dinner table. It was meant to be for one night, but I fell into a relationship with one of them. It was actually my boss at work, heh. It didn't work out, so she and I split. Sorry, Trish."

"It doesn't feel good knowing that you cannot move," she told him.

"Wow, so you're claustrophobic, huh? How does that work...for an android, I mean? Did you develop that, or was that a core feature programmed into your CPU?"

"I did not start out fearing the dark and closed spaces, but I learned to associate those things with you being away from me. They bring pain, here." She pointed to where her heart would be.

Brad stood staring with his mouth agape.

"I won't lock you away again, Tricia. I promise. The next girl will have to learn to accept you. Oh, and I come bearing gifts!"

He handed a bag to Tricia, who stood up to stretch her aching joints. She took the bag and opened it to several articles of clothing. It was very exciting for her, and she looked for where the bathroom was in the new apartment for her to change. When she found it, dressed, and emerged, she looked like a movie star, and Brad nodded in satisfaction with his work.

"How do you feel?" he asked, as she tied her hair into a ponytail and clipped in a pair of red earrings to match her fiery sundress.

"I feel like a woman, but am I allowed to leave the house now? To see the trees and interact with people?"

"Only when I'm with you, at first...I don't want people trying to steal you or pull you apart. Human beings can be very nice, but many are cruel and evil. If you go out alone, I cannot save you from them."

He chuckled to himself as it felt like a scene where a father was talking to his budding teenage daughter that wanted to go out. He hadn't taught Tricia how to defend herself, and in this new neighborhood in which they lived, there would be a strong possibility she would have to.

"Tell you what. As a peace offering for keeping you locked up, let's go out tonight. I'll take you on a date, and everyone can see my new girl and be jealous of me."

0 1 0 1 0 1 0 1 0 1 0 1

Tricia walked with Brad down the busy streets of North Avenue. It was both exciting and frightening for her as men stared and people tried to push past them. It intrigued her how humanity could be so congested, yet still work in concert to get from one place to another. The flying cars and the driving ones zipped past her recklessly, and she continued to flinch when they did that, as she expected them to crash. She saw androids everywhere, but they didn't look or behave the way she did. They were servants to humanity; awkward, mass-produced golems that drove taxis, swept the sidewalks, and much, much more.

This image of the world frightened her, and it gave rise to numerous questions that only Brad could answer.

"Why am I different?"

"How come the android over there is missing an arm and his creator won't fix it?"

"Are all androids servants to humanity? If so, then what is my service to you?"

"I look human – was this by design?"

"Why do humans allow us to be treated like this? Why aren't you more like them?"

Brad heard all these questions. Not all at once, of course, but over time she would ask them during their frequent talks or question and answer sessions. He was very proud of the way she was adapting, and while the majority of her programming was set within the base *Threerade* kit, he had done the necessary adjustments to take her from intelligent machine to damn-near-human. He could tell that she had seen the regular androids and that they freaked her out, but he kept his mouth shut so that she could absorb the experience of humanity. He wanted her to get a full dose of it, so that if ever she was alone, she would know how to handle herself.

Tricia was determined to get one of the androids to notice her, to really notice her and engage her in conversation. She tried to make eye contact with a taxi driver who sat on the hood of his car, waiting for a customer. The pale android stared back at her, but there was no recognition reflected in his eyes. Not of her similarity, no kinship nod of familiarity, nothing. It was as if he only saw a human being staring, and he tipped his hat and kept on scanning the streets for a customer.

Eventually a few androids recognized her, but no humans did. The androids would send her silent messages, asking her why she looked so different, and if her human was breaking law number fifty-nine: "an organic is not to use a synthetic for sexual pleasure." She was offended whenever one of them would ask her this, but most of them were nice, and welcomed her to their world.

One of the things that Tricia could not understand was catcalling. Brad was always playing on his personal device and would sometimes get distracted and fall behind. When he would linger she would be walking alone and at the mercy of men on the street. For the most part it was harmless, until one took offense to her silence when he called out to her.

"Baby, you look like God's gift to man on earth. Do you know that? I've never seen legs so smooth on a woman. You take good care of yourself, huh?"

Tricia had kept quiet when he said this, trying her best to understand why he felt the need to tell her what she already knew about her looks.

"It's rude not to reply when you're being spoken to girl, you know that?" He continued to press. Then he got close to her, to force her to confront him. When he gripped her shoulder to bring her around, Tricia threw up a hand to defend herself. The man's face was not fast enough to move on this reaction, and she caught his temple and accidentally knocked him out. A few women that were watching the exchange cheered for her, but Brad caught up to her and sped her away, hailing a cab as he did so to take her back home.

"I did not mean to strike him," Tricia said, as tears poured from her eyes.

"You did nothing wrong. It's my fault for leaving you alone. Look, come here." And he took her into his arms and hugged her close so that she could finish her crying and process the situation. He hoped that she would know not to do it again. "Well if there's one positive thing that came from our walk it's that everyone thinks that you are a certified babe."

"A babe? A term for—oh, so men find me attractive?"

"Yes, that is why almost all of them were trying to get your attention just now. I need you to be careful because this can become a real problem. Never leave the house without me there to protect you, and by no means are you to unlock the door when I'm not there."

"I understand...thank you for your help."

"Well, I'm responsible for you...No need to thank me for doing my duty."

"How long will it be for my hands and feet to get color?"

"I should be getting the final batch of skin next month. Don't you worry. Soon you'll be just like the rest of us skin walkers."

WITH SCHOOL A DISTANT MEMORY and work yielding the same cycle of faces he'd been seeing for a year, Brad began to feel lonely. He'd tried to warm up to Tricia—his representation of the woman of his dreams—but she was new in the world still, and because of this her questions and naiveté made him feel guilty for pursuing certain levels of intimacy with her. This did not stop him however, but he had gotten into the habit of rewinding her memory whenever it would happen. He did not want her to think ill of him or look at him in a different light.

He fell out of contact with his friend Uriel after leaving school, but he got closer to some of his coworkers at the café. During the day he would work on Tricia or surf the darker areas of the SEC. One particular night he was feeling lonelier than normal, and though he had talked to Tricia for a few hours—along with a number of other not-so-educational activities—he still craved companionship. Someone like Mika, or Susan, a spontaneous human being, one that came with her own likes, dislikes, and pet peeves. Tricia was perfect, but perfection was only ideal in theory when it came to relationships. Brad wanted a little mystery, so he decided to look into the dating services area of SEC. There was a section called *Finding Heart*, and it was one that SEC members used to setup one-night stands and love connections.

"Where do you live?" The A.I. operator asked him as soon as he opened the virtual door that had the impression of a heart on it.

"Oh no, don't worry about that. I'm just here for information."

"Are you sure you aren't interested in a list of skin providers in your area? Only the best escorts are here on SEC. No rip-off agents or abusive pimps, only men and women who wish to exchange their time and pleasures for money, goods, and services."

"I realize this, but I have no need for that – trust me. I want to look at the single girls in my area."

"Why? Shouldn't you sign up for a regular dating service and connect with other singles that way? This seems like—"

"I don't want to sign up for twenty sites, hoping that a girl takes pity on me and responds to my nudging. What I want is what you can provide; I want to be linked to girls interested in guys like me."

"The cost for that sort of service is one hundred and fifty dollars a month. Can you commit to that?"

The site was asking for a fortune just to give him opportunities, but Brad thought about it and he didn't have anything else going on to change his reality. He could pay the money and start to land dates around the city or he could continue to teach Tricia to play the part of his girlfriend, which made him feel like the world's biggest loser. The pills had built up his confidence, but his luck with women had run out. His charm no longer seemed to work, and his flirting only led to friendly conversation and not much more. He paid the operator a deposit of one hundred and fifty dollars and recorded a video of himself for his potential match to see. He was brutally honest in his description, and before long he had a profile up, and began to peruse the photos and videos of women that were provided.

"Shopping for a girlfriend, Brad?" Tricia asked as she walked over to him in his bathrobe and looked at the screen.

He had completely forgotten about her and didn't know how long she'd been watching him go through the site. "Did you not make me to be your lover? I don't understand the need for you to find a mate if I am your mate. Do you require multiple partners, or a variety of human and android lovers?"

Embarrassed by her questions and unsure how to answer them, Brad found that he could not talk for a while. *Why is she referring to herself as my lover?* Brad realized too late that after their time together that morning, he had forgotten to rewind her memory. Doing so now would prove a problem since he had taught her so much during the afternoon, so now he was in a situation that he'd hoped he would never be in.

"Tricia, this morning was another lesson for you to experience humanity. We won't talk about it any further, but it doesn't mean I built you for that reason. That would make you less than you are, and I built you to be great."

"If that was a human experience, then I must say that it was strange—but wonderful. This still leaves me confused as to why I am here. If I am not to be yours, then what is my purpose?"

"I want to make you an independent, free-thinking person. I want you to develop your own goals and aspirations based on experiences, and I want to build more like you—hopefully. You are the first in a line of new androids that I want the world to appreciate. I gave up so much to build you, but it's because you are my future. You are THE future. This is why I say that being someone's lover is not your goal. You are destined for greatness. The future Tricia will be speaking at universities, on talk shows, meeting the president, who knows..."

"Do I lack something the women on that display have?"

Brad looked over at her and her shapely legs and then it dawned on him that, outside of the outfit he had bought her, she had no clothes. "We're going to have to get you your own wardrobe," he said, glad to change the subject and press on since she seemed intent on confronting him about his love interests. "If people see you wearing my stuff all the time, they're going to think that I'm a massive pervert. Let's see what they have at Dan's emporium."

He pulled up the website, and Tricia sat next to him with her chin on his shoulder, looking on. His phone chimed and he answered it as if it were a lifeline. He walked into his room and she slid over into his seat and began to peruse the store herself.

"That was my mom checking in on me," he admitted as he came back and nudged her out of his seat. He saw the items in the shopping cart and looked at her with surprise. "I've made the girliest android known to man!"

"I've selected a few things that will allow me to look more human but at the lowest cost, Brad. The items with the notes next to them can be removed, if it is too much money."

"Don't worry, this isn't bad at all." He laughed and then accepted the charges for the items that Tricia had picked out.

She walked over to the kitchen to prepare him breakfast—a thing she had started to do without his influence, assuming that she needed to feed him since he wouldn't feed himself.

When he was eating his eggs and drinking his coffee in front of the television, Tricia snuck back onto the computer and perused a number of social websites. Human interaction intrigued her, and she was pulling in all of the slang and acronyms that the online community used. She even made herself a profile. In the past she would merely touch the CPU and be able to surf, type, and experience the internet, but Brad had admonished her for doing it that way, since "only machines can do that."

He would waffle quite often from wanting her to act human to act more like a machine, but she had decided that being more human would be better for her. One thing that stuck out the most was their relationship. Brad had obviously built her to be his mate, but even now he continued his quest to find an organic girl. It made no sense at all to Tricia.

"Be good Tricia," he said as he got up suddenly. He kissed her on the top of her head, and left the house.

While he was gone, Tricia looked at the *Finding Heart* website and took note of all the women Brad had viewed in the last hour. Considering the way she looked, and the way the women in Brad's romantic past looked, it was obvious that he had a preference for dark hair and light eyes. She wondered how long he would be, but the loneliness was creeping in once again, so she went into his room and sat on his bed, then powered herself down.

She awoke to a strange signal that droned loudly inside of her skull. It was as if someone had turned something on inside of her to make her aware, and when her eyes flicked open, she was in the bed with Brad. Her robe was on the ground, and he was asleep and shaking. The way he shook frightened her, and sweat covered his naked, muscular body. She had learned that the human body could be damaged repeatedly to evolve into a stronger, more attractive version of itself, but she had never seen Brad lifting weights or running to achieve the body he had. She could smell the alcohol on him, and it was obvious that something had happened while she was recharging on his bed. She felt his arm and it was cold and clammy, and he did not seem well at all. She laid back down next to him and powered herself down, hoping that when she woke up again, he would be okay.

"Morning, Trish," Brad said after he got up, showered, and walked out into the living room. His eyes were bloodshot, but he seemed relaxed and happy in comparison to how he'd been the day before.

"Good morning," she responded. "I have a question for you."

"Sure thing. What?"

"You seemed sick last night when you were sleeping. I've never seen you that way. You were cold and shivering, and your skin felt the way plasticine does when I am powered down. You also—"

"I know, and I'm sorry. That wasn't right. See, the pills have a bad side to go along with the good side. I've been hallucinating and having dizzy spells. To counter the effect I've had to take other drugs, and let's just say that last night I felt as if I wanted to die."

"Have you run an analysis on the pills you have been taking? What if they contain something that could cause long-term changes—"

"Hey, Trish, let's not go there. I made a deal with the devil and I'm going to stick with it. Knowing the details is not going to make this any easier for me, so I would rather not, okay?"

0 1 0 1 0 1 0 1 0 1 0 1

A few weeks later Brad made a love connection. Her name was Priscilla White and she was a dancer. She had reached out to Brad after she recognized him from the coffee café, and they'd begun calling one another every day. She was a performing artist who specialized in ancient African dances and she invited Brad to see her perform. He thought about taking Tricia but worried that it would confuse things for Priscilla, so he went against his earlier promise and powered her down before locking her away in his closet. Priscilla was brown-skinned and had short curly hair. He found out that she was from Trinidad, in the West Indies. She liked watching horror movies as much as he did, and they shared a love of coffee.

The show was at the performing arts center at the University and Brad felt embarrassed at having to return there. He hoped he wouldn't run into anyone that he knew. If they realized he was no longer a student, they might wonder why he was still hanging around the campus. He tried to put it out of his mind as he sat in an empty row towards the middle of the auditorium. There weren't many other people there to watch the performance, so he was relieved that he wouldn't have to sit directly next to strangers.

The show started and a number of girls came out to the music, kicking high and shimmying this way and that. He didn't see Priscilla so he opened up the program that had been handed to him at the door and scanned the names to see if he could find her. Priscilla White was the last name on the list, and so he tolerated the show for a few more minutes. As soon as he was at his breaking point and was ready to get up, she appeared onstage. She was dressed in an outfit that made the other performers look like nothing and the people in attendance clapped loudly. Apparently this particular show had her as the main event, so he was happy to see her, even though it meant he had to sit through the entire dance performance.

Once the show was over, Priscilla met Brad by her car and they stood outside talking for a long time.

"Are you aspiring to be a professional dancer?" he asked. It seemed like the right kind of question to ask, but as soon as the words came out of his mouth, he felt stupid for asking them. *Priscilla had her degree and was working; shouldn't it be obvious that the dancing was a hobby?*

"That would be awesome if I could, but no. I like what I do and I'm a little too old to be pursuing that. Not to mention the pay isn't that great for dancers, not unless you're with the big names. They don't want girls my age, trust me."

"Your age? You're like twenty-three. Is that considered old for professional dancers?"

"No, but it's too late in the game for that sort of career change. So, did you like the show?"

"Oh yeah, you were amazing. There were people on their feet cheering for you, and I can tell that you are the one most of them came to see."

"Look at you, you flatterer. Thank you!"

He spoke with her some more before she got into her car and drove away. He was even more attracted to her now that he had seen her dance, and he went home happier than he'd been in a very long time.

The next day she came into the café and ordered a cappuccino. He didn't take the order since he was heating up a customer's pastry. He saw her in line and she winked at him and he didn't know how to react to it. When he made her drink he used the machine to place a heart inside of the foam. He called her name and she came up to him and he told her there was a surprise inside.

"A surprise? What did you do to my drink?"

"I put a little something extra inside. Take a look."

"Let's see," she said. She opened the lid and smiled. "Aww, is that a heart?"

He nodded and looked around to make sure that his manager was not within earshot. She sat down and did some work on her computer while Brad stared at her whenever he could, looking away quickly whenever she would catch him. He loved her confidence; she was everything that he wasn't. He liked that she knew how he felt about her but didn't get creeped out or resort to games like many others would. Near the end of his shift she turned off her computer and walked up to him to let him know that she was leaving.

"Would you like to come over tonight and watch a movie?" she asked. "Maybe have dinner?"

"I would love to," he replied as they strolled out to her car. But he couldn't help but feel a little déjà vu with the Mika situation of the past. He got in his car and followed her home, and they arrived at a new apartment complex.

"Welcome to the mansion," she said playfully.

He hovered behind her as she walked to the door and let him in.

"What do you do for work?" he asked as he removed his shoes and sat at her bar.

"I'm a pharmacist. Uh, and I don't cook alone, so get up, come over here and start chopping up these carrots."

He loved her personality and the way she could playfully make demands and he just had to comply. She was making shrimp fried rice, so she had him handle the vegetables while she did the cooking. When they were finished she handed him a bowl with a decorative set of chopsticks. They settled down on a mat in front of her television to watch an old, classic movie by the name of *Splice*. The movie was about two scientists that played god and developed a genetic mutant from several animals. The mutant grew into a beautiful girl with a scorpion-like tail, and due to the way she was raised by her scientist parents, she began to transform into something else completely. It struck a chord with Brad and he wondered if Tricia was undergoing the same thought process as the creature Dren in the movie.

When it was over Priscilla was laughing and wondering why Brad looked as if he had been scarred.

"Well, that was freaky," she said as she prodded him in the ribs. "This movie proves that guys will sleep with anything."

Brad thought about the mornings when he would wake up next to a powered-down Tricia and wipe her memory. A wave of sadness overtook him. "I feel sick," he said before thinking better of it.

"Oh, no, did the food upset your stomach?"

"No, the food was great. You're a brilliant cook. It's just that movie was a little disturbing y'know? It really made me think, and it speaks to how messed up we humans are."

"You're such a nerd, Brad. Only you would find the intelligent, big picture in that weird thriller."

She got up and collected his plate and he used her bathroom to wash his hands and face. There he was in the home of a beautiful pharmacist but despite his new confidence and her friendliness, he didn't know whether to kiss her, or take things slowly out of fear of her running away. Splice had put Tricia on his mind and he felt cruel for creating her only to discard her whenever he got into situations with other women. It was out of rage and hurt that he'd developed her into a beautiful woman, and he'd had ulterior motives he would have acted on if the pills hadn't changed his luck with real women.

Tricia was in a closet that would be her home for a time until he worked up the urge to tell Priscilla. How would he break it to her? He stood at the sink for a long time, thinking things through until she popped her head in the doorway.

"That movie really got to you, didn't it? Can I get you something? I have ice cream and we can watch something else. Just let me know."

"I'm okay, really. Thanks for a great time. We should do this again—"

"How about Friday? Do you work on Friday?"

"No," he lied, and thought of what his excuse would be to call in sick that day.

Priscilla was sexy, and he had never dated a girl like her before, so he looked forward to seeing her again. They had the same sense of humor, liked the same movies, and she teased him constantly which made it easier for him to be himself around her. She was almost too good to be true.

When he got home, he found Tricia out of the closet and seated on the couch, watching television. She seemed confused and looked at him as if he were a stranger. *How did she get out?* She watched him as he entered, but said nothing to him as he looked over some discarded dishes in the sink.

"I went out with a beautiful girl today, Trish. She cooked for me and we watched a movie."

"Should I be congratulating you?" she replied sarcastically, and then got up to stand in front of the mirror to do her hair.

"I'm sorry for lying to you about the closet. I panic sometimes when I think of how people will judge you, and call you names—"

"Are you worried that they'll do that to me or to you?"

"Touché..."

"You've changed, but I don't think that you understand the change. As your android I have watched you transform from a bashful, kind individual, to a dark, cocky version of yourself."

"You need to say nicer things to me unless you want to spend more time in the closet."

"Don't bother," she said and then walked back into the dark closet and shut the door.

She powered herself down and went to sleep and he stood watching her, feeling powerless and stupid for his empty threat. When she awoke, she was back in the bed next to Brad's sleeping body. *How did I get here?* She wondered, *why is this becoming a recurring thing?* When she had asked Brad about it a few weeks ago, he had said that he wasn't laying her in the bed with him. If she was the one voluntarily doing it, she would have it in her memory—yet she didn't. Brad muttered the name "Priscilla" and rolled over to embrace Tricia's body tightly and this further confused her. She couldn't stay upset with him, but she wondered about his erratic behavior and the memory lapses that had been occurring.

She decided that she would do something about it, as she suspected that Brad's change was more than what she was experiencing. She slid out of his arms and pulled on a robe as she went into the living room to find the pills.

0 0101010101101

The next time Brad saw Priscilla she came by his apartment to get him. It was spontaneous and unexpected, and he wondered what would have happened had she seen Trish, or another woman in his place. When she called him to tell him she was there, he quickly threw on some shorts and a shirt to check if she was lying. When he went outside she was at the base of his stairs, and she was dressed as if she had been jogging.

"I was in your neighborhood so I decided to check in on you. There aren't any girlfriends in there that will beat me up for calling you, are there?"

He laughed at her joke, and then despite his better judgment, put on some tennis shoes and joined her on her run. Exercise was foreign to Brad, but he gave it his all and they took off on the sidewalks of the busy street.

"You do this all the time, Priscilla?"

"What, pop up at people's houses like a stalker?" She grinned. "I jog every morning, but I don't typically come this way, so consider yourself special, sir."

He was pleased to hear that she had detoured her route for him, and though he struggled to keep up, he felt lucky to be in the company of a pretty girl. After about a mile he felt as if his chest was about to explode so he stopped with his hands on his knees and Priscilla jogged back to check up on him.

"Aww Brad, you aren't a runner, are you?"

"Does that disappoint you?"

"No, but you should really exercise. Come on, we'll walk the rest."

When they got back to his place, Priscilla pushed him inside and pointed to his bedroom. "You need a shower buddy; you smell a little funky."

He popped her with his rag playfully, which resounded in a satisfactory squeal, and then he hopped into the shower as she'd commanded.

While he was in there, Priscilla walked into his bedroom. "Hey Brad, I'm really tired," she said and he peeked outside the bathroom door to see her playing with the statues on his counter.

"I'll be doing laundry tomorrow. You can sit on the bed and rest till I get out."

He hoped that his invitation didn't make her think him a pervert, and he hoped that Tricia would remain hidden and powered down so that there would be no issues. Even the accusation of a human owning an android for relations outside of work came with legal ramifications, so losing Priscilla romantically would be the least of his problems if Tricia revealed herself. After about twenty minutes, he walked out of the bathroom in an old jogging suit that he wore for leisure. Priscilla—who had taken him up on his offer—was on the bed asleep, and her legs hanging off the side let him know that the exhaustion had gotten the better of her.

I have a beautiful girl in my bed, he thought, and wondered how it was that he was so lucky to have the privilege of hanging out with her. He shook her awake and pointed to the shower, but she shook her head and groggily asked him to drive her home. When they got to her apartment the tables turned, and she went to take a shower while he looked through her video files for a movie to pass the time. He found a catalog of new releases, selected one, and started watching it. He was starving but he didn't feel comfortable enough to raid Priscilla's fridge. When she finally made an entrance, she was in a flowery frock, her hair wrapped with a matching bandana.

"You look like a Carly Venice video," he said, referring to the young pop singer who prided herself on dressing like the neo-soul divas of the 1990s.

"Shut up," she said, smiling, because she took it as a compliment. She sat next to Brad, who was showing no interest in the movie. "I'm starving, how about you?" she asked, and it was as if she could read his mind.

He drove her to *Benito's*, a Greek eatery, and then they walked to the liquor store so that she could buy some Chardonnay, and then back home to her apartment. It was late, and they finished the movie while eating their leftovers and drinking wine. At one point Brad looked over at her and saw how shapely she was in the light of the television, and wondered if it was appropriate to sneak a kiss. She was obviously interested, having spent an entire day with him—part of which was in his bed—but he didn't want to chase her away.

"What?" she said as she turned to him smiling.

"Oh, nothing. Just looking at you. Sorry..." he said, embarrassed that she'd caught him staring.

"It's alright Brad. You can look at me. Today was nice. I like hanging with you."

He didn't realize how tired he was, but by the time the movie ended he was asleep on the end of Priscilla's couch. When he woke up, he had a comforter covering him and a pillow beneath his head. Priscilla's bedroom door was closed, possibly locked, but it was dark everywhere, and the bright blue numbers on the clock below the television read 4:15 a.m. He went back to sleep, and then woke up to the sound of Priscilla walking around.

"Good morning, light weight," she teased him, and he ran to the bathroom to release the urine that he'd held for over an hour so as not wake her.

"Want a bagel?" she asked when he emerged. She spread cheese and tuna on hers.

"I'd love one, but crap—I'm supposed to be at work."

0101010101010

The next week while walking the aisles of a grocery store, Brad saw Mika, who made to wave at him until she saw Priscilla walk over and place some food into his basket. Priscilla had them shopping for the meal she would prepare later. They were going to do their customary movie night, and she wanted to make tacos to go along with it. He didn't know why it mattered to her who Priscilla was, but it seemed to affect Mika's mood, and she turned to keep walking, as if she had never seen him. It was a small victory in his head, especially if his wishes had come true and she was now single and regretting the way she'd led him on.

Brad and Priscilla had gone through two movies when he decided to put in *A Hero's Redemption* by R.F. Chambers. It was an independent film that explored the life of a couple made to live with one another in a small, secluded house. He sat next to Priscilla on her couch, and while every urge in his body was to pull her in for an embrace, he worried that doing so would end their new friendship, so he kept his hands to himself. This was their third movie night in two weeks, and nothing had transpired past a few playful touches, and a hint here and there. His heart was racing, sitting next to her, and she had gotten so comfortable with him that she wore a nightgown and had pulled her legs up on the couch.

He kept trying to steal glances at her through his peripheral vision, but she would catch him every time and then offer up a small smile that he couldn't read to save his life. Things got really uncomfortable when the main character in the movie had a sexual encounter, and the director decided that it needed an entire ten minutes to play out in graphic detail. Brad, without thinking, brushed his hand across Priscilla's thigh and she paused the movie and stared at him, shocked.

"Why did you do that?"

Because you are irresistible, he thought. "I thought I saw a bug on your leg. It was a reaction."

"Ooh, I think I see a bug on your arm," she said, and she thumped him on his arm with a big grin on her face.

He brushed her thigh gently again, and this time she relaxed her legs and leaned back a bit. He took the invitation and got closer to her and kissed her lips. The movement was awkward, and he kissed her the way one kisses the cheek of a relative, or a close friend. This prompted further teasing by Priscilla, and she took matters into her own hands and kissed him deeply. They kissed for a time, Brad still afraid to let his hands roam where he wanted them to go.

"It's about time," Priscilla said after they'd been kissing for a minute. She snuggled into his arms and they resumed watching the movie.

Brad wished that he was braver, as he would have had gotten further into things with the willing Priscilla. He felt the evidence of his body being ready, but his brain still held on to the fear of rejection. "About time?" he asked.

"Yes, I was wondering when you were going to kiss me. We've been going out for weeks and you never even tried, so I was beginning to think there was something about me that was making you wait."

Brad turned red with embarrassment. What did she want him to do? Push up on her and act like some sort of aggressive sex fiend? No, he wanted her to know that he respected her so, like a gentleman he had waited for her approval. She felt good against his body, and as the movie went on he grew more and more confident. By the time the credits were rolling, they were kissing again, and this time his hands made their way to places he'd only dreamed about touching her.

"You should go home now before I do something I'll regret," she said.

"You should do it, anyway."

"I'm sure you'd like that, wouldn't you? But, it's late, so you should go home."

He leaned in and kissed her some more, but she was strong and walked him to the door and locked him out. It had been a wonderful night, and this was evidenced by the big smile he had on his face as he walked out to his car. The taste of Priscilla's lips was still fresh on his mind, and it was hard to think about anything else. His vision seemed cloudy and hazy, but he had been drinking, so he squeezed his eyes tight and opened them, trying in vain to sober up as he found his car and headed home.

Inside the apartment, Tricia was missing and he looked in all of the closets before turning on the lights to find her asleep on the couch. The haziness of his vision passed and he kissed her gently on the forehead before going into the bedroom. What was he going to do with her? Should he introduce her to Priscilla now, so she would be aware of his life's work, or should he wait until they were further into their relationship? *It was a relationship, right?* He asked himself as he laid on the bed, staring at the ceiling.

When he awoke, Tricia had ironed his clothes for work and had them arranged on the counter. He looked around for her but she was nowhere to be found. He had a momentary panic attack as he thought that she had run away. It was only when he found her powered down in the closet that he relaxed and could breathe again. The fact that she would voluntarily hide herself and power down in the closet made him sad and sick with himself. He lifted her into his arms and brought her to the couch, where he laid her down and cried. *I have been the biggest jerk to you Tricia*, he thought, and then he wiped his face and headed off to work.

0101010101010101

Tricia pulled her hat down low as she walked along the busy sidewalk, doing her best to avoid eye contact with anyone. She found the drugstore she was looking for and went inside and sat in the waiting area. She was alone, and the pharmacist she had been talking to on the phone finished up her shift and came out to meet her.

"Tricia?"

"Yes, hello, Jolene. I hope this isn't too much trouble?"

"No, not at all. I am very interested in this pill you were talking about. Did you bring the sample?"

"Yes, it is right here. One tiny pill that made my mas—I mean, my brother gain confidence. I think it is doing more than that though, and if you can let me know, I can either warn him or get rid of them."

"Wonderful. I'll take it home and analyze it, and then I'll call you and let you know what I found."

"You're very kind. How much do I owe you?" Tricia asked, even though she knew that she didn't have any money, and would have to find a way to get some from Brad secretly.

"Probably nothing, but let me see how much work it will be first. If it turns out to be some *Zenine* or *Drencyn*, I won't charge you anything."

Tricia had gone against Brad's wishes and left the house. But with his wavering moods and the increased time that he kept her powered down, she no longer felt it was in her best interest to listen to him. There were lapses in her memory too, and whenever she would wake up inside of his room, it was as if she'd been re-wired to forget how she had gotten there. Living with Brad was one blackout session after another, and when she was coherent and with him, they were arguing, and he was threatening to lock her away.

The Brad she knew from the past would never treat her so cruelly, and she wondered if it was due to his mysterious new girlfriend that he was acting the way he was. She walked back to the apartment slowly, letting the sound of the city and the contact with the people embed into her memory banks for the times in the future when she would be locked away. Jolene would look into Brad's pills for her, and though he was almost out of them, he'd said he would order more, and the Japanese would be more than happy to keep him supplied. More pills meant more neglect and abuse by the new Brad, but if she could fix him then life would return to happier times. Brad had been lonely, and the pills had helped him to become more attractive. Though he had built her to be his friend, the pills now made him see her as nothing but a nuisance.

"Hey beautiful," a middle-aged, balding man said to her as she walked past a small mall entrance.

"Are you talking to me?" she asked.

He came over to her, adjusting his tie. "Anyone ever tell you that you look like...erm, what's the actress? Judy Pops, the one that was in *Lady Hellgate*? I think you look better than her though—"

"Thank you, but I have to leav—"

He grabbed her hand to keep her from leaving, and smiled as he squared up with her while taking her other hand. "Don't run off so quick, Judy. I just want to talk to you. Do you have a man?"

"Yes, yes I have a man."

"And he lets you walk out here by yourself like this? What kind of man is that? I would never let you go it alone."

"Could you please let go of my hands? I have to go."

"Alright, alright. Can I have your contact code? We should hook up later. You don't act like you're from around here. I can take you to a nice restaurant. I'm telling you, the one I have in mind...they have the best rib-eye."

"No, thank you," Tricia said, and she walked away from him quickly, crossing her arms over her chest to stop her breasts from bouncing, and keeping her head low to avoid any other would-be suitors. *I must not come out alone again*, she said to herself, and when she got near her apartment complex, she ran inside and locked the door.

Stepping into the apartment after her traumatic encounter, Tricia began to notice things she had looked past when she was still confined there. The place was a dump, and Brad hadn't bothered to straighten up the way he used to when he was a student. The classic neat freak now had sketch papers everywhere, and the kitchen held discarded dishes from days past. There were half-finished beers and what appeared to be two bowls of old fried rice. There was a noticeable stench of rotted food coming from the kitchen, and a roach scurried across the wall. So Tricia proceeded to clean it all up and put the place in order. She would not allow Brad to make her into a servant-droid like many of his friends had, but she knew that a clean house would help his psyche, so she got right to it.

4 | WILL YOU BE MY GIRLFRIEND?

"SO, WHEN WAS THE LAST TIME you were in a relationship?" Priscilla asked as she walked hand in hand with Brad around the artificial lake.

"Oh, well—er, a year? She and I really weren't, well she stopped taking my calls about a year ago. Is this a relationship?"

"Well after last night, it had better be. I don't let just anyone spend the night, and I trust you, so... I want you to say it."

"Will you be my girlfriend?"

"Yes!"

A trip that had started out as one of their standard dates had quickly become one of the best days in Brad's life. He and Priscilla had kept on doing movie nights at her house after the day Tricia had cleaned up, but she wouldn't sleep with him, at least not until last night. Tricia had gotten better about his frequent absence, and he left her to take care of the house when he was away—especially since he practically lived with Priscilla, whose home was amazing. He found it strange that after visiting his home and commenting on how "cozy" it was, Priscilla seemed unwilling to hang out there or ask him questions about it. So he spent most of his time at her place, eating her food, watching her television, and being with her.

The routine would go as follows: he would go to work in the morning, stop by the gear shop to sell a few rotors, and then drive to Priscilla's house in the evening to hang out and sleep at night. He had been doing this for two months now, and Priscilla didn't seem to mind. Rotors were what he called the tiny, flying robots he made from excess mechanical parts. He had gotten better with artificial intelligence, and began to hustle the little toys for extra money to supplement his small barista's income. Career-wise he viewed himself as a failure, and he struggled internally with whether to reveal the genius of Tricia to the world or to keep her as his personal secret.

Tricia's revealing would get him arrested, at least for a time due to her illegal parts. But she would revolutionize modern robotics, and he would be on every talk show across America. After the talk shows, he'd be approached by a private company and they would throw millions of dollars at him to replicate the process. Tricia would cease to be special, and would more than likely be disassembled and reverse-engineered. This latter fact made him not want to do it. She was a person, a person he had built, and he didn't want her murdered and dissected for money. But being with Priscilla brought the pressure of wanting to do more. There would be outside competition from men that had a lot more than he had, and could do a lot more for her than he could. *There is nothing special about me. I'm just a broke, coffee pusher*, he thought. So it was out of fear that he'd begun selling rotors.

It had crossed his mind to make another Tricia, but this time keep the A.I. restrained, and remove the ability to freely think from it. The idea could work, if not for the skin he couldn't afford, and the things he had done during groggy nights— things that he didn't write down or store into memory. The truth was, Tricia was a brilliant mistake. The day he'd walked in and saw her dancing was the day he realized this. Androids didn't do that; they didn't crave learning like human beings did, and they didn't get upset when their masters spent more time with their girlfriends than them. Sometime during the hacking of her A.I. and the installation of foreign parts into her frame, he had found true intelligence. He could pretend that he had the means to do it all over again, but he would need a new Mika to break his heart, several drugs to keep him awake for days, and the luck he'd had when she came to life.

"Let's go to *Celia's* tonight to celebrate!" Priscilla said as she rested her head on his shoulder.

He could hear the happiness in her voice, and it was because he had committed to her. The fact that he couldn't afford Celia's Steakhouse didn't matter to him. He had to find a way to afford it. How sobering would it be for him to remind her how poor he was when she had just become his girl? The situation depressed him, but it wasn't enough to interfere with the pride he felt in having a girl—a very special girl—as his girlfriend.

As if she was reading his mind, Priscilla whispered into his ear, "It's my treat. I just feel like a steak right now."

She would be paying for dinner and it made him feel emasculated. Would he be one of the many guys across the nation dependent on their women? Both parties should be pulling their weight. Or, as his father had drilled into him from the time when he was a boy, "*A man provides*". Yet here he was, a man, and the only thing he was providing for Priscilla was conversation. He felt small, and the urge to impress her and prove his worth pushed him to start talking.

"I—I have something I need to tell you, Priss."

"What's up, baby?" she called him baby, and the sound of it made him even more comfortable in talking to her.

"I have an android. Not the kind you can buy and assemble, or rent from the cleaning companies, but true artificial intelligence. She's very convincing as a human, and way ahead of anything that we have right now."

Priscilla stepped in front of him on the sidewalk and her mouth dropped open in an expression of awe and happiness. "So you're a droid engineer?" she asked excitedly, and he couldn't understand why it made her so happy.

"I never got my degree, but yes, I can build androids. Tricia, the droid I'm telling you about, was my first try at it, and she is brilliant. I can take you to meet her, if you'd like."

"No, it's okay. Androids scare me a bit, to be honest. To hear that you've built one to be so real, well, she would give me nightmares.

Don't get me wrong, I'm all for technological advancement, but what happens when she gets too upset, or malfunctions due to coming in contact with a network virus or something? She could kill you. I think that it's so hot that you're like a mad scientist genius or something, but knowing is good enough for me. Let's go get some steaks. I'm freaking starving."

While Brad considered the paranoid, technophobia to be a massive letdown on the part of Priscilla, he felt more comfortable with her paying for his meal after she perked up about his passion. She was content in knowing that he had great potential as an inventor, and now he would just have to actually work at it instead of sticking to his poor life of mixing coffee and watching television. Her fear of androids also meant that there would be no future for her and Tricia in the same vicinity. For now he would have to keep Tricia at his apartment and continue to stay with Priscilla. In time she would come around, especially after seeing how wonderful Tricia was—at least that's what he hoped. But for now life was good, and he had a real girlfriend.

010101010101

"Tricia, how long has your brother been taking these drugs?" asked Jolene, the pharmacist. She had a worried tone in her voice and it let Tricia know that she had bad news.

Brad had been gone for a few days, and while it was okay that he'd gotten serious with Priscilla, it was unlike him to stay out so long without checking in. He had taken the pills with him, so the plan to switch them out or destroy them all had been delayed.

"He's been taking them for over a year now. When they run out he orders more."

"I'm sorry for what I'm about to tell you, but there may only be a short time to help him, if he's willing to listen to you. The pills have a chemical in it that is known to affect the brain. It makes you feel confident and free in your thought, but it causes damage in the long-term. People have died, developed personality disorders, and much, much worse. You need to stop him from taking those pills, and check him into a hospital where a doctor can assess his condition. This is really bad Tricia, and I would advise you to destroy the pills...they would be illegal here, and we don't want people reselling them to make money."

"Thank you so much," Tricia said. "I'll find a way to do what you say. How much do I owe you? It sounds like you did a lot of research to get me this information."

"It's no charge, hon. Just look after your brother. Give me a call if anything comes up with him. This whole thing has piqued my interest, and if there is anything else I can do to help, please don't hesitate to ask."

Tricia thanked her once again and hung up the phone. She began to search the house for the pills, and when she found them she destroyed them. She thought about how easily he could order more, so she hacked into his personal computer and logged into his email to find the correspondence. His dealer's name was Abe, and his email seemed to be routed through several layers of security. She created a new account on a free email server, and made the credentials similar to Abe's and coded in an automatic response algorithm. Whenever someone would email his account, it would respond with one of a thousand unique messages that indicated that the pills would be on their way. She then changed the alias "Abe" in his email history to be the one that she had just created, eliminating the real Abe completely. Lastly she sent an email to the supplier, telling him that she was Brad's sister and that he had died from a fatal accident.

It took several hours for Tricia to shut down or reroute all of the ways Brad could use to get more pills. She knew he'd be persistent, but the things that she had done would be impossible to detect.

Despite Tricia's attempts to sabotage Brad's drugs, the last thing he had on his mind were the pills. He was with a girl that liked him, he had come up with a plan to mass produce his rotors, and even though he spent as much time as he could with Priscilla, he knew that in time he would go to see Tricia and clear the air between them. He sat at Priscilla's table, watching her as she practiced her dance routines in the living room. She was everything he dreamed of, and he couldn't believe he was right there with her, free to love her, touch her, and see her practice the thing that she loved. How could he tell her she was his first love? Priscilla had been his first where the heart was concerned, and he couldn't get her out of his head, no matter how hard he tried.

He thought about high school, and how he had wanted to end his life. Mom was the one who'd talked him down from the virtual ledge, and she was the one that had always cared. *Mom...when was the last time I called my mom*, he thought, stunned at how absent-minded he had been, and he looked at his personal device where he had blocked her contact during a fit of rage. *That was several months ago. Why did I forget to unblock her?* He hopped up and went out on Priscilla's balcony, and clicked the icon to call his mother.

"BRADLEY?" A surprised voice screamed into the phone, and he heard her whisper to his father that he had called. His father had cut him off from money and communication with him—as if this would magically make him re-enroll in school and resume the path of a physician.

"Mom, I'm so sorry I haven't called you guys. I've been depressed, you know. This whole decision with school and whatnot...but I got better, and I'm working to be an entrepreneur now. So—"

"We were worried sick! Your brother said he went to go find you, but you'd moved and didn't tell anyone where you were going."

"Tell him to stay away from me. I have nothing to say to that ass—"

"Bradley, he's your brother!"

"And dad is my father, and they're both money-hungry douchebags with an elitist complex. I called for you mom, because I love you, and I want you to know that I'm okay."

"Oh, my son, that is really good to hear. We miss you so much. When can you visit?"

"Soon, Mom. But listen, I have a girlfriend! Can you believe that? And, and she's pretty too... I'll show you." And he got up and snapped a picture of Priscilla kicking her leg up in front of the television as she emulated the dance moves on a video.

"She IS pretty Brad. I am so happy for you. What's her name?"

"Oh, sorry, yeah, her name's Priscilla! Priscilla White, and she's a dancer and a pharmacist."

"I can't wait to tell your father. A pharmacist, you say? He would love that."

"He'd probably love the fact that she's black too, right Mom?"

"Don't start. He's getting better about that."

"He's a piece of work. But anyway, I'll call you again, soon. I promise. I miss you."

"I love you, son."

He hung up the phone and sat in silence as he thought about his parents. His mother was an artist that had fallen in love with a stiff doctor who came from a long line of doctors. He was also a conservative bore, with ancient beliefs in racial and class lines that dated back to the third Great War, and he tried to instill them into his children. His brother, Patrick, was the golden boy that had failed. He went to school and did everything that his father wanted him to do, but couldn't take the pressure, so he changed majors and graduated to make menial wages. He was a bully, and everything Brad remembered about him from when they were growing up was Patrick doing everything he could to make his life hell.

He walked inside where Priscilla was taking a break from her dancing and snuck up behind her before she could react. He wrapped his arms around her waist and rested his chin on her neck, and she smiled from ear to ear as he swayed with her as if music was playing and they were dancing.

"Who were you on the phone with?" she asked. She turned to face him and put her arms around his neck.

"That was my mother. I hadn't spoken to her in ages, so I was checking in. Plus, I had to tell her about you, and how I was the luckiest man in the world."

"Stop being so sweet. Maybe I'm the lucky girl."

"Are you practicing for another performance?"

"Oh, I do Carnival every year. I'm going down to Miami next month so I have to prepare my costume and figure out what I want to do before then. The dancing is to get me into the mood for the Calypso festival. You should come. I can dress you up and we have a good time at Carnival."

"That would be great but it's too short noticed. I wouldn't be able to get off work. How long would you be gone for?"

"A couple of weeks. I have family there who want to see me, so it would be a trip to visit, plus dance all night like we do every year."

The thought of losing her for that long made him anxious, but her smile helped him keep his cool and accept it. He hadn't taken a pill in three days, but he didn't feel any less confident than he did when he was taking them daily. *Maybe I could spread them out more, and save myself some money from reordering them all the time*, he thought. He had sent the final journal of the effects to the Japanese a while back, and through his results—along with several others—they had put the pills up for sale on the black market.

"Earth to Brad," Priscilla teased, with that song-like accent he couldn't get enough of.

"Sorry, I was just thinking. Been a lot on my mind lately."

"Well I was saying that I need to go in to work. Will you be here when I get back or do you have some errands to run?"

"I'm gonna check in on my apartment, and build out a few more rotors. Call me when you're getting off, and we can get dinner or something."

"Okay sweetheart, I'll give you a call." And she kissed him before retreating to her room to change for work.

Brad was walking on air. If someone had stopped him to tell him how scruffy and worn out he looked, he wouldn't believe it. Priscilla loved him, and that was all that mattered for now. Without his pills he had begun to smoke marijuana to calm his nerves. *To think that pot was once illegal in the United States of America*, he thought as he smiled and took in the high rises and the flying cars that zipped this way and that on their designated airways.

Hell, alcohol had been outlawed at one point, too. Now the vices that were outlawed were even stranger: there were laws against loving and marrying machines—which brought in the need for android restraints. There were laws against littering, which carried some of the harshest penalties. Tricia, in terms of what he meant her to be, was an illegal android. If the authorities knew that she existed, he could get up to a month's time in jail. He knew the risks and it made him paranoid, but for a young man with a foxy Trinidadian girlfriend in the city of Seattle, life—at least for the moment—was grand.

He strode along the sidewalk towards the café but his mood started to darken quickly. He didn't know what had come over him, but he wasn't feeling "good enough" for the world. He wanted to crawl into a corner and hide, to get away from people, bills, and Priscilla's judging eyes. What was he thinking about? She couldn't be serious about him; any day now she would tell him it was all a joke, a bet to see if she would willingly date a loser.

He skipped the café and found a bar. There was a basketball game on and a bunch of excited old men that looked like they spent most of their time there. Sitting down near the corner, he asked the bartender to give him a shot of rum, and he nursed it and thought on his miserable life.

By the time he was finished he was seated on the curb in front of the closed bar. The streets were emptying out, and the droid patrol was asking drunks like himself if they needed a ride home. He dragged his tired body home to his apartment and vomited in the toilet. Tricia—who was quite surprised to see him—helped him clean up, and then she gave him several pills to help him get through it.

"I need my pills," he said to her, and she stared at him as if confused. "Pills, Tricia. The Japanese ones. They're in that closet over there. Get em for me, will you?"

She walked slowly to the closet and grabbed the bottle to bring it out to him.

"Thanks, Trish, you're a life saver," he said to her and swallowed one quickly.

Tricia watched him to see if there would be any recognition of her having switched the pills out for store-bought headache relief. He sat still for a time as if he expected a reaction, then moved to the couch and switched on the television before motioning for Tricia to join him.

"Why did I have to make you so hot?" he said to her in a drunken stupor.

She looked at him with disgust. She'd never dealt with a drunken version of him before.

"I wonder, can androids get drunk, or high? We HAVE to program that into you if you can't, Trish. You have no idea what you're missing."

"Why are you talking to me that way? Is your head feeling healthy?"

"It's 'is your head feeling okay.' 'Is your head feeling okay?' You haven't been practicing your speech much, have you?"

"How can I when you are never here to talk to me?" she replied angrily.

He gave her an odd look and smiled, then lifted one of her hands and kissed it. "I'm sorry I talked to you like that, Priscilla," he said, and before she could correct him, everything went black.

When Tricia powered on after the blackout, she found herself alone in Brad's bed. It was the same situation as before. She could only remember the earlier part of the day before, and she was in a bed that she would never voluntarily lay in. Machines did not need beds, and while she could lay in one to emulate human behavior, standing up or sitting down to power down was quite acceptable. She heard a loud groan and a few expletives from the far side of the bed, and found Brad seated on the floor, looking around, confused.

"What the hell are you doing in the bed?" he asked. "Christ, my head is pounding, and I feel like crap."

"I cannot remember anything. I think that there is something wrong with me. Every other day it seems, I reset, and I wake up in your bed with memory loss. Was this programmed into me?"

"Why would I even want to do that? Look, you're beautiful – I made you that way, and part of me loves the fact that I woke up next to a beautiful woman this morning, android or no android. But, this is how misunderstandings start, and if Priscilla came in and saw you like that, I'm toast. Wait a second, we didn't... did we?"

"I don't understand what you're asking."

"Nothing. I'm a bloody fool. Look, I'll check out your brain as soon as I shower, okay? You shouldn't be experiencing blackouts, just like I shouldn't be drinking and feeling like a pile of dirt right now."

She got up from the bed and dressed herself, then went into the kitchen to make him a pot of tea. The blackouts were concerning, and she wondered if it was a flaw in her design due to Brad's inexperience, or if he was lying to her for some reason. She only experienced them when he was around, and when she woke up, he was always there. A part of her knew what was going on but she wanted to believe that he was being honest with her.

"I'll be better about coming home to talk to you," he said to her, and with her forgetting their argument the night before she took it as a good sign that the loving, caring Bradley that she had started out in the world knowing was on his way back to her.

WHILE BRAD WAS GENERALLY HAPPY when he was with Priscilla, he was a completely different animal when it came to her being around other men. Brad hated the way that average people behaved, but in a closed-in setting, he felt like they got worse. Men would push up on women they saw with weaker men, and if they weren't strong enough to keep them at bay, those weaker guys would end up alone by the end of the night. So when Priscilla showed up with tickets to a college basketball game that she had scored from a coworker, he was not very excited to go.

"Don't you like sports?" she asked.

He hesitated in giving her an answer. He felt funny telling her no. It was one of those loaded questions that brought into question his manhood, and normality, that he knew she didn't realize was a bit offensive.

"Of course I like sports, everybody loves sports," he lied, but she was insistent and eventually he caved.

She dressed in jogging pants and a tank top representing the home team, but he decided to wear the same jeans and t-shirt he was in. She looked at him as if he was hopeless when she saw this, but took it in stride as they headed out together, hand in hand, and happy. *It won't be so bad*, he told himself as they stood in the slow line that flowed into the building. The outside of the auditorium looked like the classic bowl shaped arena that had carried sports since the age of the Roman gladiators, but inside it was a marvel of modern engineering.

"This is a college auditorium?" he asked Priscilla as they walked around the lit corridor that bordered the raised stage. Floating ads popped up in front of them as they made their way to their seats.

"You're definitely not a sports fan, are you? But that's okay, baby, we can work on that," she said as she pinched his cheek playfully. "This is the auditorium for the Supersonics! If a college team had anything near the level of this thing, I would assume the city would have a fit."

They sat in their seats and Brad exhaled in relief. The anxiety of walking through the crowd had put him on edge. Priscilla rested her hand on his thigh and he lifted it up to his face and kissed it gently. She looked over at him and smiled, then snuggled into his arms. The announcer shouted out declarations of grandeur for the two teams as they began to file onto the court to begin their warm-ups.

Soon the game started and Brad was actually enjoying it as the teams were quite competitive and the players showed off their tremendous skills. He smiled and clapped when someone sank a three-pointer or slammed the ball over someone else, but Priscilla was on a completely different level of hype. She was on her feet screaming, pumping her fists, and becoming quite emotional when their team was down. The whole display should have been obnoxious, but to Brad and a number of men in attendance, it was quite cute and attractive.

One of the men that saw her bouncing up and down with glee couldn't take his eyes off her, as if she had a spell on him that he couldn't break. Brad saw him staring and began to stare back, making sure the man knew that Priscilla was his and he should find someone single to leer at. The man saw Brad staring and smiled at him, recognizing the sort of pathetic jealousy that came with a pretty girl. If Brad could have seen himself he would be disappointed and upset, but he had taken some pills before they headed out, and he assumed that this was him being confident.

Brad tried to bring Priscilla in close to let her admirer see that she was with him. This action brought around an annoyed Priscilla who looked to see why Brad wanted to be close during a time that didn't warrant it. First she looked at him with a slight question in her smile, then she looked around to see who was seeing them being clingy—which was a point of embarrassment for her—and that was when she saw her admirer laughing at the exchange.

"Are you serious, Bradley?" she asked, shocked by his behavior. The home team was being demolished, so she motioned to him for them to leave. Brad was more than happy to get out of there, but Priscilla was quiet and walked ahead of him rather quickly. As they walked out of the coliseum he grabbed her hand and spun her around so that she had to look at him.

"I'm sorry, I don't do well with crowds and that guy was looking at you like he—"

"Like he what, Bradley? Like he wanted to sleep with me? Guys are going to look at me, and I don't want you trying to fight all of them for it. You're a sweet guy so don't act like the jerks I used to date, please."

He liked the way she called him Bradley; it was almost her pet name for him, just like "Priss" was what he had for her. The moniker came from a popular children's cartoon that Brad had watched and loved as a child—even though he would still tune in whenever it was on. Prissy Missy was the name of the title character, and she was a sassy black detective with super powers. Brad loved the art and the veiled adult humor, so when he heard Priscilla's name, it was the first thing that had gone through his mind. The jealousy was stupid, but he would be lying if he said that he would ever be okay with another man looking at her.

"It was stupid," he said as they slowly walked to her car, she in front, him trailing behind.

"What's stupid?"

"My actions just now. I'm not sorry for staring that guy down for his wandering eyes, but I am sorry for getting you mixed up in it by trying to pull you in to kiss me. You are the most beautiful girl I know, so of course people are going to stare. I'm just not used to it; this is all a new experience for me."

"I'm still mad at you but I won't lie, you make me feel like a queen. You're different, and this is why what you did just now is so not you. Who cares if some creep stares at me? We all have eyes and I didn't even notice it. Life is too short to be so petty."

She didn't understand how Brad felt, but being with her was like being on guard duty all day long against the men of the city that overstepped their boundaries. It was the same with Tricia, and he had grown accustomed to stepping up when necessary. He felt silly for his actions at the basketball game, but if he hadn't done that the guy would have made it a point to come over and talk to her.

They found a cozy little shop off the beaten path to get some espressos. Priscilla ordered a Danish to go along with her coffee and Brad had a shot of espresso by itself. They sat on the outside and continued their conversation, while sipping away at their drinks.

"All my life, I've seen smaller, smarter guys have their girlfriends taken away by big buffoons that liked to talk. It made me realize that I would be fighting an uphill battle with women throughout my lifetime," he finally said.

"Really, Bradley? You should give us women a little credit. Any woman that gives up a good man for someone like that is a fool in her own right. I think those smart guys are better off without them. I'm not a fool, so no need to go trying to fight people for me."

He nodded. "How's work?" he asked, wanting to change the subject.

She let him. "Not bad, actually. Our IT department stinks, and I find myself doing my own troubleshooting daily, but that's all I can complain about."

"What sort of troubleshooting? You know that's my area."

"Look at you trying to play the hero again. Bradley, you got this." She motioned at her entire body with a gesture that was almost seductive. "There's no need to guard, hold-down, or fight anyone over me. I'm your girl, alright? Plus you haven't noticed the way other women look at me when we're out. I could easily assume the role of overprotective mate, too."

"Other girls give you looks?"

"All the time. It's pretty funny to me the way they flash hate in their eyes."

"What's funny is that if it were me alone at these places, those same girls wouldn't look twice at me or give me the time of day. It's just how people are. Upset when you're with someone and they aren't. It doesn't matter how that someone looks to them. It's all so damn silly."

The table was small, so they were extremely close even though they sat across from one another, and Priscilla leaned in for Brad to kiss her. They stayed like that for a time, letting their kiss erase the embarrassment of the earlier hours during the basketball game, and refocus them on how they felt about one another. People that walked by and saw them locked into this kiss merely smiled, dispelling their earlier thoughts that singles disliked all couples that showed public displays of affection.

They walked the town afterwards, taking in the people and the general atmosphere of the Seattle nightlife. They went into a bar to get a few drinks and the mood lightened when Priscilla got a little tipsy from the beer. They were at a high-top table in the rear of the near-empty bar and she was giggling uncontrollably. Everything was a joke, and the volume control seemed to break in her voice box as she cackled loudly and became a bit obnoxious.

"CAN YOU EVEN FIGHT, BRAD?" she asked, and he looked around to see who had heard her.

"Of course I can fight."

"When was the last time you got into an actual fight?"

How about we take it back to the car, Priss? I think you've had enough."

"No, I'm okay, babe, just having a laugh. Calm down, relax. You're too uptight."

He looked at her to remind himself how lucky he was to be with her but suddenly there was a flash of bright light, and he saw Tricia looking at him, plain as day. Then her face blurred and he was on the floor of the bar, looking around.

"Brad!" Priscilla was yelling. She came around and helped him to his feet as he held his head and looked about, wondering what had come over him. Priscilla smelled good, so he hugged her close, and took her outside where they walk-stumbled until they found a bench to sit on and watch people walk by. The night air felt wonderful. It was chilly but not to the point where it was uncomfortable, and the sky was clear, its darkness broken only by the large white orb of the moon.

He sat and watched the people walk by while Priscilla fell asleep next to him. He wasn't tipsy or drunk so he wondered why it was that he had blacked out and fallen at the bar. No one had made to help him, except Priscilla, who wasn't in much better shape than he was. He let her sleep for half an hour before shaking her awake and helping her back to the car. They'd had enough excitement for one night, and while he had wanted to spend more time with her, she was worn out, and couldn't do much more. She was leaving for Miami the next day, and they had argued. He wanted it to be different, but all he could do was drive her home.

01010101010101

The black car pulled up to the front of the red brick building and detective Homer Montgoya parked it down near a tree and waited. It wasn't often that a violator of rule 59 presented himself, and he wondered what manner of pervert he would see exiting the house. He pulled up the warrant and shook his head at the charges. The front door of the red brick opened, and Professor James Leroy Anthony stepped out. He was stopped by a beautiful woman who adjusted his sweater vest and kissed him on the cheek.

"Well, if anything, I gotta say the old man has taste," Montgoya muttered to himself as he exited the vehicle.

He crossed the lawn at a brisk space. He raised his stun gun at the man. "Mister James L. Anthony?"

The man turned around, surprised to see the police officer on his lawn. "Yes, I am James Anthony..."

"You are under arrest for the crime of mechanophilia. Please turn around, get on your knees, and place your hands on your head."

"I will comply, officer. What crime have I committed—besides the assumed—for me to get this level of embarrassment at my home? I am a proper citizen, and a professor. Who would make these accusations against me?"

"You're a pervert, professor, and our government doesn't want perverts in society. Think about it for a minute, will you?" He cuffed the older gentleman and stood him up before dusting off the dirt that was now on the knees of his corduroy pants. "Men like you professor, brilliant men who train the geniuses of the future, should be populating the earth with your seed. If our beloved government allows you all to choose machines over warm, breathing human beings, who would produce more men and women like you? The spice-heads and drunk losers of society?"

"I appreciate your kindness, and gentleness in this detective, and I overreacted as none of my neighbors seem to be up yet. I wouldn't like the gossip, since none of them know about my beloved Constance. It isn't...perversion. It's—it's a long story."

Montgoya placed him in the passenger seat, ignoring his safety protocol so that the people who would see them would assume the professor was a friend and not a criminal. "It's a long drive back to the station, professor, so why don't you explain it to me. Look, I can't change our laws, no matter how absolutely stupid they are, but I want to understand. What makes a man love a machine?"

"We all have our reasons, detective. There is no grand organization of robo-lovers where we swear off partners in lieu of androids or anything like that. My personal reason came about when the love of my life died from the cow disease. Marcy was my partner in everything, and a brilliant engineer in her own right. When I lost her so suddenly my life was in shambles, and what came of it was a partner that would not be vulnerable to diseases, poisons, or the cruelty of our humanity."

"How long ago did you build her?"

"We've been together five years now. The government has been hypocritical about machines and what we can and cannot do. The military androids are not given restraints, and have routinely shown the human traits of PTSD, trouble adapting to civilian society, and much, much more. Is it not evident that with intelligence, even a machine can be cared for? Or do we need another long age of prejudice and ignorance before we realize that we are wrong in our limitation?"

"That's too deep for me, prof. I'm just a simple cop doing his job. What I don't get is that the perverts who lust after our kids are given treatment and set free—void of their functional parts, of course—but we put guys like you in jail for months at a time. I would love to let you go, delete the paperwork, and pretend that I never saw you, but I guess you haven't been watching the news. You're part of a large scale crackdown on robo-lovers."

J.L. Anthony sat back quietly and thought on his long career. They would lock him up for a month, and he would lose his job at the University. Even worse, they would take Constance away from him. She would be restrained, and her memory wiped, then she would more than likely be converted into a servant. The tears fell from his eyes as he thought about life without her. She was his everything, and even though the detective was nice and respectful, he couldn't stop what would become the end of a long and illustrious career.

"I appreciate you talking to me and hearing my side, detective. You have a kind heart, and I wish you a long and prosperous career—
"

"Whoa, don't be so morbid professor. You sound like life itself is over. You know that all of this is a political show, right? Some schlep is running for governor and wants to show the religious-types that he's all about the sanctity of good 'straight' relationships. Consider it a month's vacation, and then afterwards you get to go back to your life of pencils and mechanics."

"I wish it were that easy young man, but even an android cannot be replaced when love is involved. I am truly sorry." He pushed open the door and jumped. They were on the topmost highway which was well above the tallest buildings in the city, and before Montgoya could react he was plummeting to his death. He fell through the midlevel and lower highways, smashing into cars as he did, and was dead before landing in front of a crowd of people looking to cross the street. The fall brought about a chaotic stampede of panic. People were not used to seeing someone die, let alone someone falling from several stories above on the secure highway.

"Ah, damn it!" Montgoya yelled, as he thought about how he would explain the old man being in the front seat.

He shifted gears and made to land, but there would be no explanation for the suicide. For all he knew, he was in a world of trouble due to the professor's decision. J.L. Anthony was a legend in the robotics world, and his death would bring about a large discussion on androids. People would once again question why the laws against loving an artificial human were so harsh and wonder if the police department executed him. On top of that, the fact that many people saw the professor's wife being an android as a minor, personal thing meant that his suicide would be deemed unnecessary and a fault of the police department and their government puppet masters.

0 1 0 1 0 1 0 1 0 1 0 1

When Brad had shown the professor his progress on Tricia, the old man had beamed with pride. At the time, Brad thought his excitement was due to him going above and beyond on the assignment, but Dr. Anthony was elated that Tricia was similar to what he had done with his wife, Constance. After the suicide, the internet went ballistic. Every other country had feedback on the United States' record of repressive laws. Everyone knew that religion was to blame for the country's motivation and old arguments resurfaced in the community.

The death, and the fact that the professor had an android for a wife, brought out android activists. They rallied for Constance's release to them, since androids in a case like this would be sent to a chop shop to die. The peaceful city of Seattle turned violent and young people flooded the streets in protest, refusing to comply with the police until Constance was freed. Brad, tearful and saddened at his mentor's death, joined in with the protestors and he took Tricia with him. It was the first time she had been outside in a long time, and while the cause was important, she glowed simply by being a part of the experience. She loved having the opportunity to fight for her own rights.

Every day they would march out there with signs that read "HYPOCRITE!" and scream at the police that tried in vain to keep order. Occasionally the police would fire canisters into the crowd, which would emit a white smoke that made them feel sleepy, and quiet them down for a time. People began to wear masks, and things heated up, even resulting in a few people getting shot.

After a week had passed, Brad seemed tired of protesting. He had been talking daily to Priscilla while she was away and when she came back in town he disappeared from Tricia's side to see her. He was so excited to see Priscilla that he told Tricia that she could freely come and go as she pleased. When he left, Tricia took the opportunity to walk around the city. One day she walked for twelve hours straight, taking in the high-rises, the quaint coffee shops, and the young vendors inside of them. It made her wish she was human, so that she could not only taste the treats inside, but hunger for them as pleasant memories of places that she'd visited.

It was late in the evening when she rounded the block of a nice neighborhood and saw a large red brick house bordered by electric wire. The slight touch of the wire would shut her down immediately, so the sight of it frightened her and she quickly crossed the street to the other side. As she did this she began to hear a loud pinging noise inside her head that was unlike anything she had ever heard before. The pinging got louder and more painful the further she went away from the fence, so she got near it again to reduce the pain. She looked around to make sure that no one was observing her odd behavior. *Please, help me*, a soft voice echoed in her head, and she wondered if the fence was meant to find droids and pull them to their deaths.

She closed her eyes and answered the voice; it was a new way of communicating for her that she did not realize she had. *The fence will kill me if I get near it, who are you?* She asked.

The fence grew dark for a time before the voice returned. *Hurry inside. Hurry! I can only keep it off for a few seconds.*

It was night now as Tricia looked around, and the fear of being assaulted or kidnapped took over as it always did when she was outside. She slipped through the gate of the fence, hoping to gain access to the red brick house.

She ran towards the front door that was left ajar. When she got inside and locked it behind her, she knew immediately that it was J.L.

Anthony's house. There were awards and photos of him and his beautiful wife everywhere, not to mention half-finished androids, and large textbooks. She walked the long hallway that held these photos and followed the signal to a pair of doors. When she opened the large double doors to a massive study, she saw Constance, wife to the late J.L. Anthony. She was standing in the center of the room, looking tired and worried.

"What is happening outside, girl?" Constance asked, her voice sounding nothing like Tricia had expected. "I saw them arrest James, but he didn't call, didn't send word. Then when I tried to go find out myself, I saw that they had erected an electronic fence to keep me in."

"Why didn't you just power it down like you did for me just then?"

"The trick is to use my own transmission to trip the device that keeps the fence powered. Unfortunately, there is a price for me doing that. First, I cannot move, and second, it drains my power immensely. Even now, I feel light in the head, and I need to rest to recharge soon. So answer my questions, quickly please. What is going on with my husband?"

"Have you not been watching the news?"

"I have, but I refused to believe any of it. Why would James kill himself? They say he did it because he was ashamed of me. That makes no sense!"

"It doesn't make sense because the media is lying. Your husband chose to leave this world because they were going to ruin his life and destroy you in the process. They arrested him for mechanophilia, and he would have been fired from his job in disgrace. They intend to power you down and restrain you, but many humans are rioting the city to make sure that you aren't treated unfairly."

She gracefully walked over to Tricia and hugged her tightly, and as Tricia returned the gesture she couldn't believe how good it felt.

"I felt you, when you walked outside of our house. I felt you, and you felt like me. We are the same, you and I," Constance said as she held her. "We were built out of love, and were built to love. The only flaw in our design is that without love, we are nothing. Your maker. Is he a nice man? Does he love you? Are you a happy wife to him like I was for my beloved James? You look so sad and tired, my dear. I am beginning to think the worse."

"My maker is kind but he neglects me. He is confused and out of his mind due to stress, drugs, and I think there is a woman. He leaves me alone for many days, and when he is with me I have blackouts that remove my memory. Sometimes I sneak out and walk amongst the humans but this has proven to be dangerous. I get along well enough, but I keep worrying that I will have a blackout and someone will kidnap me and discover what it is that I am. Brad tells me not to go out without him, but how can I just sit around doing nothing all day? I cannot stay powered down, no matter how hard I try. It's driving me—"

"Let me take a look at you," Constance said. She moved her hands around Tricia's head and did what she could to access her CPU. "Your maker may not be who he appears to be, girl. The world as you see it now may not be what it is. I can assure you that I am real, but for how long you have walked to get here, and the reason why you managed to find your way here...those reasons may not be clear to you. Do you know what day it is?"

"Tricia, my name is Tricia. It is Thursday, January 11th."

"Tricia, it is May 8th. You have no internal clock. This was removed when you were created. Your maker did everything he could, it seems, to make you as human as possible. But he did leave in a rather frightening feature."

"And what feature would that be?"

"Are you positive that Tricia is your true identity? Do you have any memories of another persona, perhaps?"

"What do you mean by that? You are scaring me. What did you see just now?"

"Oh Tricia, I am sorry, but this will not be easy. I think that when you were created, you were created for a different purpose than the one you have been playing out for your maker. I see that you're still confused but don't stress; I am patient and I want you to get it. Let me explain to you what it means when an engineer removes your restraint."

BRAD DROVE OUT TO PRISCILLA'S APARTMENT COMPLEX and ran up the stairs to surprise her. With Tricia's help, he had sold enough rotors to buy her an engagement ring and the plan was to make it a date night. After dinner at *Celia's*, he would fall to one knee and propose. It was too fast, and he knew it, but he didn't want to take any chances in losing her, especially with his ongoing dark moods. He placed his card against the door but it flashed red instead of the familiar green. *Come on, why isn't it working?* He asked himself. He kept on trying before knocking loudly on the door. He heard footsteps running to the door and he forced a smile as he adjusted his tie and straightened his shoulders to greet her.

"What do you want?" an old woman said as she came to the door. She looked tired and sleepy.

Behind her and inside of the apartment Brad could see a sleeping old man, and the walls had an ugly wallpaper that made the place seem ancient.

"P—Priscilla White, is she here?" he asked, confused.

The old woman shook her head and slammed the door. He checked his key several times to make sure that it was right. 153B that was the number on the door he stood in front of. He tried a few doors adjacent to it, and was met with either hostile residents or nice ones that felt sorry for him. He ran back to his car and looked for her contact code to call her.

"Why can't I find her in here?" he asked out loud as he scrolled up and down his list of contacts, all to no avail. "This isn't funny. THIS ISN'T FUNNY!" he yelled, and then punched the steering wheel until his knuckles were bruised.

There is no way that a person can up and vanish into thin air. He looked at the apartment buildings, which were not as nice as he remembered them and there was no sign of Priscilla's car in the garage.

"This is so freaking weird," he said.

He drove to his apartment. It was quiet and clean, the way Tricia had left it when she had gone off on her stroll. He turned on his computer and began to browse for the correspondence that he would have had with Priscilla. But it was as If he had dreamt about the entire year of pleasure he had with her.

A day's worth of searching to find Priscilla turned into panic as Brad began to remember what it was like to live without her in his life. He needed to be reassured of his sanity, to know that Priscilla was merely playing a prank and that they would be reunited within a day's time. *Maybe Tricia knows something*, he thought as he pulled open the closet door and flipped the light on to see her. The lights came on to an empty room, and he looked around as if she had somehow snuck behind him.

"Priscilla's gone and now Trish. What in the hell is going on?" he asked out loud, as he went to every door within his apartment and pulled them open, hoping to find his android.

Tricia was gone, or she had been stolen. But as unfortunate as that was, the bigger issue was that his very human girlfriend was gone without a trace. He tore the place apart for hours before falling on his bed, exhausted. He recalled a time when he was at Priscilla's house and she was dancing. She was always dancing, but this particular time was special. He had called his mother, and he'd uploaded a photo to her. The memory snapped him back into reality and he called his mother, skipping the greetings to ask if she still had the photo.

"Photo? What photo, Brad? I haven't heard from you in a long time. You never call your mother. What is going on with you?"

"I'm fine, Mom. It's just that my girlfriend has disappeared."

"Disappeared? Like kidnapped, disappeared? Have you called the authorities? You know many girls have been coming up missing lately."

"No, I haven't called the cops yet. Tell you what, Ma, let me talk to you later. I'm gonna call them."

Brad hung up his device and went into the kitchen. The pills had stopped making him feel confident and calm like they used to and he couldn't understand it. His emails to the Japanese contact were mostly ignored, and the ones he did answer were canned lies about the order coming in soon. His body was craving them, but he had used them all up and had no hope of refilling his supply. To make up for the way he was used to feeling, Brad began to drink and ingest nasal-spice whenever he could afford it. The spice made him jumpy, and there were segments of his short-term memory that was missing. It hadn't mattered much to Priscilla that he was his old, awkward self, but he didn't like being that guy. He was depressed, and dark thoughts were again clouding his thoughts.

He called the police and put in a missing person's report for Priscilla. He was crying on the phone, and he didn't realize that he had poured himself a drink as he sat at the table. He tried to shift his focus to where Tricia was, but the loss of Priscilla was too strong to put out of his mind. He thought about the tracker that all android kits came with, but he had removed it from Tricia's frame. She was fully autonomous but very much like a child when it came to safety. If someone had broken in to try and rob him, they would have found the beautiful android asleep in his closet.

Unrestrained, advanced androids were illegal to own, but this did not stop gangsters and pimps from kidnapping them and selling them into prostitution. Androids were not as vulnerable to the STI's, mental trauma, and aging that a human being was, so high-level pimps would run out android girls. Tricia was a sophisticated build that could fool anyone that she was human, so the price she would go for would be remarkable. If this was her fate he would never see her again.

The police let him know they would keep him updated on the case, but this was not enough for him so he drove out to Priscilla's apartment again. He staked it out for hours even though his hunger made him want to give up. It grew dark and there was still no trace of Priscilla coming or going. When his phone rang he expected it to be the police telling him they found her. But what he got instead was his mother.

"Hey, Mom."

"Brad. I found the picture you sent me. I'd saved it to show your father, so I am sending it to you now."

He placed the device into the internal matrix of his car, and the windshield darkened and became a replica of the device's screen. A photo popped up of Tricia dancing in front of the television like the day he saw her and promised her skin. The photo was new to him, and he didn't remember taking it, or watching Tricia dance in the skimpy outfit that was in the photo. *Was I high?* He asked himself. He sat stunned, staring at it, wondering why it was he couldn't remember.

"Is that her, Brad? She is very pretty. Your father bragged about you to his colleagues for a whole month when he saw that picture. Did you call the police? I really hope that she is okay."

"Wrong girl, mom," he said sadly, and his heart began to race as he wondered about his memory lapse. Why was it so vivid in his mind that he had taken a photo of Priscilla and sent it to his mother? They had even discussed her nationality, and—*why was it all so vivid?*

He hung up with his mother and then called the café to ask if he could have the morning off. Susan answered the phone as if she was surprised to hear him, and when he asked her to get time off she laughed as if he had told her the best joke in the world.

"Of course you can have the morning off Brad, you hilarious, junkie loser. Do you not remember walking out on us last week? Tell me, your highness, how was sunny Trinidad? I'm not sure how you rich, party types get down on vacation, so if you could share some of your stories with me, I'd love to hear them."

He hung up on her and hit his head with the heel of his hand to see if he could jog his memory back into commission. *Am I still smart?* He wondered. He began giving himself complex math equations to see if he could still solve them. Without brains, how good was he to anyone? If he couldn't remember quitting his job, and which of the two women in his life he'd sent photos to his mother of, he was that much closer to becoming a moron. He began to cry again as the fear of losing everything loomed even closer to reality. His eyes found their way to an old pill bottle. He had loved the way the pills had made him feel. They had brought Priscilla into his life and allowed him to take Tricia to a level that no other android he knew of had attained.

Without the pills he hated himself, and without Priscilla, he had no love and support. Depression reared its ugly head, and he sat drumming the table rapidly with his fingers. Losing Priscilla felt like losing several limbs, but without Tricia—his life's work, and his sign to the world that he was somebody—he felt no reason to go on. He had to find Priscilla; he had to know that she was okay.

So without planning or thinking better of it, he packed a bag and headed out to investigate.

0101010101010

Tricia opened the door to the apartment, expecting to find it clean and orderly, the way she left it. But what she found was chaos. Brad had torn the place apart and she assumed that he had been looking for her. She hoped he was okay and that he wasn't running the streets looking to see if she was in trouble. The rioting had still been going on in the streets but the government decided it would be in everyone's best interest if Constance was restrained but released to the activists—

with a tracker and probationary check-ins to make sure she stayed restrained. The move had prompted Tricia to shorten her stay, and she had run back home in order to avoid discovery. The activists were okay with the decision, so things settled down in Seattle. On a worldwide scale however, the fighting continued for the rights of humans that wanted to love their androids.

When she flipped open the computer to track the history, she saw where Brad had searched several engines and databases for the name "Priscilla White" and came up empty-handed. She saw where he had hit the wall, where his tears had fallen, and she felt saddened that he was going through the sort of pain that he was. She decided that she would find a way to help him, but first she had to find him and she didn't know where to start.

Constance had given Tricia a sizable sum of money to help her to become more independent in the world. It would allow her to go places and do things that she couldn't before. One of these things was to hire a private detective, and she found her way to the office of a Mr. Homer Montgoya. He was a former star detective on the police force who had been fired for unknown reasons. Tricia knew of him because of his commercials on television. He was a robo-rights activist, and as the commercial said, he could find anything if the price was right.

She walked inside the small plaza in the late afternoon, and approached his tiny office once she made out the badly designed sign that read "Montgoya P.I." He was clean-cut and had really nice black hair that was rather unique due to the pattern that his gray hair grew within it. He was in a well-tailored suit and old-style black and white wingtip shoes. A large and genuine smile crossed his tanned face as he stood up to greet her upon her entry.

"Senora," he said to her without breaking the smile. She nodded and took a seat in front of his desk. "My name is Homer Montgoya. What can I do for you on this lovely afternoon?"

"Thank you Mr. Montgoya. My name is Tricia. I have a friend that has gone missing. Her name is Priscilla White. She is very pretty, has brown skin—"

"Do you have a photo of your friend, Miss Tricia?"

"No. Is it possible to find her without a photo, or would it be hopeless?"

"Where there's a will, there is a way, Tricia. So she's a black girl, your friend?"

"Yes, and she's about my height—I think. She is Trinidadian, and she has an accent, and I think she works for a local pharmaceutical company."

"That is a good start."

"Shall we discuss your rate?"

They sat talking business for thirty minutes, and when Tricia left, she felt confident that Montgoya would find out something. She turned her efforts toward finding Brad—who had recently disappeared to look for Priscilla—so she went to the café and asked around. She didn't know that he had quit working, and it made her wonder if he'd found a job doing the thing he actually liked doing—creating. She went into the bar he frequented and then to the places she knew that he and Priscilla liked to go to on their dates. Her search came up empty, so she went to the public library where he used to hang out.

Tricia did not find Brad at the library, so she took the opportunity to find a computer and look into the strange behavior he had been exhibiting. She wanted to have a cure for the pills when she found him, so she looked for a condition that matched up with his. While she found traits of his behavior across several different conditions, she could not find one that directly correlated with his behavior. The entire mystery of his change was irritating and unfortunate, so Tricia doubled her efforts and took the internet into the dark, underground avenues where only hackers, black hat masters, and deviants lived. If she could not find his condition in the public-facing web, perhaps she could find it in the alleys.

She flipped past pages of pedophilia, terrorist cookbooks, and anti-government rhetoric, searching for Japanese threads about the little black pill. She found a blog that was owned by someone who calling themselves *BuStream*. The entries were sporadic and varied in length, but they were written well, and had commentary by other people who were on "the system" as they called it. She flipped through his archives until one caught her eye:

The Ultimate High
By Author BuStream

Black lightning is unlike any other drug I've ever taken before. You all know that I've taken them all, felt them all, been there, and done a lot of that. Lightning makes the rest of the drugs look like cheap dates compared to her: long-lasting, all-consuming, demand of you attention. When you're on it, you get cocky, like real cocky, and it becomes all about you. I've seen lightning riders do some strange things, all in the spirit of fixing their messed up egos.

One dude was a slob, never did anything with his life—except drugs. The lightning made him think that he was CEO of a large company – it was hilarious. This dude would sit at his computer desk shaking, screaming at his "sales people," making imaginary phone calls, and fully going through the motions, day after day. The lightning takes you over; it gives you a reality that your mind needs in order to stop you from hating yourself.

I know what you're thinking after reading this. What's the point, right? Well, lightning is genius. Imagine if you can placate an entire nation with these pills while you come in and take things over under them? It's not like they will push back, they will be too caught up in their private little worlds to care. You could give it to lifers in prison and let them carry out their sentences without violence. Lightning is illegal now, but once it becomes available to our government, it will change everything.

The mystery drug was called lightning, and it altered the user's reality. Tricia wondered if Brad remembered her, or the good times they'd had together. She looked to see if anyone had successfully come back from their time of being on lightning, but even BuStream's posts became crazier and crazier as the time went by. His writing became erratic, and the commentators all seemed to know it as they posted things like, "you've lost it man, you need to find some help." She found many other blogs and forums for the drug, but no one who had kicked the habit and returned to normalcy.

She got up from the computer and walked outside to take in some fresh air. The fate of Brad's situation broke her heart, and she could feel the tears on her face before she could fight them back. Constance had asked her about her own feelings, if she wasn't upset with Brad for bringing her into a world where he was ill-prepared to love her, take care of her, and commit to her. The question had struck a chord with her because she was upset with him. The long periods of loneliness had been traumatic, and she had told herself that she would not allow him to lock her away like that again.

The last time he tried, she had gone on the walk to find Constance. She didn't know it at the time when she set out, but the news about the professor, coupled with the activists seeking to protect his android lover, had made her want to find Constance. She had not met any of her kind that were truly intelligent—most had their restraints locked in place and couldn't communicate any more than a few pre-programmed words. Like herself, Constance had an ever-evolving CPU, learning, and growing as time went on, and it felt so good to talk to her.

She walked back home from the library and hailed a cab that took her back to the apartment. Brad was home and on the computer, moving files and photos around, and he looked – and smelled – as if he hadn't showered in days.

"WHERE HAVE YOU BEEN?" he screamed at her. He jumped up out of his seat as if ready to fight.

"Looking for you. Are you upset with me?"

"You had me worried sick. Priscilla vanishes into thin air, and I can't even find the android that I screwed my life up building. How did you get powered on? I stored you in there."

His words hurt and angered Tricia as she tried to process what he had said and determine if it was due to the psychosis from him being off of the lightning.

...the android that I screwed my life up building...

...the android that I screwed my life up building...

...the android that I screwed my life up building...

To think that he truly believed that her creation was the reason for him being a failed engineer was ridiculous. He was the one who'd dropped out of school to first become a drug-addicted barista, then quit his job to basically become an unemployed drug addict. She couldn't excuse him for saying the hurtful words to her so she lashed out.

"You didn't lock me up. Your memory is fried. Even if you tried, I would not have let you! Did it ever cross your mind that your precious girlfriend left you because you are a drug addict?"

"I am not a drug addict. Don't call me that. It's not nice."

"But blaming me for the bad choices you've made in life is? Shouldn't you take responsibility for your own life?"

"You didn't answer me. How did you get out of the house?"

She thought about what she was going to say to him but her anger placed her into a mode that was too sarcastic for hesitation. "Priscilla released me," she said with a smile. "Yeah, Priscilla came over here a long time ago and saw how you locked me away. She powered me on to ask me a few questions. She didn't think to power me off when she left, or lock the closet that you had me in, so I escaped. She seemed pretty upset—"

"What did she ask you?"

"She asked me why you built me to look the way I did, and whether or not we fooled around."

"So, you led her to believe that I was a mechanophile then?"

"What do you think? I told her the truth! Do you think the memory wipes would stop me from figuring it out?"

Brad's temper had settled down as he took in Tricia's words, and he sat back down to power down his computer and think about things. He smiled at her and nodded, and then sat back with his arms crossed as he evaluated things. Tricia calmed down, walked over and sat next to him. She touched him on his forearm and was surprised to feel how dry and unhealthy it felt. It was obvious that he hadn't been eating, and it was worse now that the love of his life was missing.

"I am going to help you find her, Bradley."

"You are?"

"I need you to promise me that you will make an attempt at taking care of yourself so that when she does return, she won't be completely turned off by your appearance."

"I'm sorry for yelling at you and for everything I've done to you Trish, but you gotta understand. The pills... the pills gave me everything. For the first time in my life I was able to meet new people, to be attractive to women, and to function out in society. I didn't second-guess myself, I wasn't looking to build friends out of mechanical parts to make up for my own deficiencies. The pills led me to Priscilla, a girl I could never dream would be interested in me, and they led me to teaching you to be so sharp. You are so advanced, and smart, and—"

"Do you hear yourself? You are giving credit to a drug that Hoshi Tan gave you to be his guinea pig. It gave you confidence, yes, but at the price of what, Brad? Are you sure that it isn't hurting you, making you more depressed than you believe? You have changed, trust me, and as your creation I would know this more than anyone else."

"Changed? What do you mean, changed?"

"You are a really mean person now, and you are obsessed. The things that you say to me, your mother, and anyone else that loves you are evidence of the pills having a downside to them. Your entire life has become about Priscilla, to the point that even now when she's gone, you are unable to let us back in. This is why I want to find her for you, but I do it in hopes of having the old Brad back, not the one that came about as a result of the pills."

"I don't like the old Brad very much. If you think about it, the way I thought and let people push me around was the reason why I built you. Not that I regret it. You are the best thing that has happened to me besides my first love, but you were built out of anger as much as you were built out of love. Your creation validates me; it lets me know that I did something that a lot of people are either too scared to do, or lack the resource and intelligence to do. You are a walking, talking sign of my potential, but unfortunately for someone like me, that isn't enough."

"What if you learn that Priscilla left voluntarily? If she came to a point where she decided that she no longer wanted to be with you, but didn't have the strength to break up with you? What will you do then? Will you just give up, let your life continue to go to shambles, and neglect me and everything else that means something to you?"

"I don't want to think of that right now. It just seems like a really dark place that I don't want to go right now. I've lost so much, and Priscilla was my future. With her gone I—"

"There was a time when you told me that I was your future. I think you need to go back to that thought process, Brad. You built me to love you, and I do. I think that you need to stand up and get back to form, and in the meantime, I will help you find your missing girlfriend."

DETECTIVE MONTGOYA WAS PERPLEXED. He had been looking for a woman named Priscilla White, but all evidence came back as if the girl didn't exist. If she had been murdered or kidnapped, the perpetrators would be professionals. What would professionals want with a young, Trinidadian dancer? She didn't seem to have money; there were no trails leading to parents in the country, and aside from Brad, nobody knew her or interacted with her over the last few months. The dance troupe she supposedly was with said they had never heard of her, and the building she allegedly stayed in had no records, either. He thought about the hot brunette that had brought the case to him, and he wondered if he was being set up, or made fun of by one of the guys at his former job.

He had been let go unceremoniously, and it was a ploy to shake the press after the suicide by the doctor. Money had dried up, his wife threatened to leave him, and his health had come into play after six months of unemployment. It was after he watched a classic film about a private investigator that he got the idea to go into business for himself. Almost immediately, he had people employing him—apparently there were a number of people missing all over the city. He wanted to find Priscilla White so he could add her as another success story in his job portfolio, but the search seemed futile, and it made him question the validity of the case itself.

Reluctantly, he pulled out the tracker he had attached to Tricia on their meeting and followed the map to where she was located. He parked outside of Brad's apartment, cut his lights, and waited there to see if she would emerge with Priscilla White, since she was obviously lying to him. The time passed and nothing happened, save for lights flicking on and off periodically and a few nosy souls coming up to his car to see if anyone was inside of it. He slept there for the night and woke up to find a skinny, longhaired junkie exiting the building.

"What's a bird like her doing with that loser?" he muttered to himself.

He watched as Brad looked this way and that. He followed him for a time as Brad walked around the city, looking everywhere as if he was searching for someone. Montgoya was intrigued, so he stayed hidden, and kept up the stalking even though he was hungry and in desperate need of a hot shower. By noon Brad seemed to tire of searching and retraced his steps back to the apartment where he went inside and shut the door. Montgoya took some notes to go along with a few photos he had taken, and went home to shower and sleep.

The next day he called up Tricia and lied to her that he had found something and that she needed to come to his office immediately. Tricia sounded confused at his phone call but agreed to meet him and came into his office in the evening.

"Hi detective," she said to him as she walked in and sat at the chair that faced his desk.

"Let me ask you this, sister. Is it just boredom, or is it some sort of deep, twisted agenda? Why you would pay me to go on a search for someone that doesn't even exist?"

"What do you mean, she doesn't exist? She's as real as you and me. Brad was getting ready to marry her, and—"

"Brad? You mean that cotton head that I saw sniffing around town as if he lost his soul or something? So, you hired me off the word of a junkie? Let me be square with you – that isn't too smart."

Tricia grew quiet as she wondered how she would move forward with Montgoya. Priscilla had disappeared like Brad had said, but she was no ghost, or made-up thing like the detective thought. Whoever had taken her, or locked her away was good, and had found a way to remove her from their reality without leaving evidence behind.

"Perhaps the problem is you, detective, and your wild boast that you are the best private investigator in Seattle. I have given you a month and I have received no updates, no calls, and no evidence that you didn't just sit there behind that desk day after day, lying about looking for Priscilla. Have you been enjoying the free money I handed to you?"

Montgoya was offended but he liked her fire and her willingness to go toe-to-toe with him in an argument. "That's a pretty nasty accusation. If you were a guy I'd punch you square in the jaw, do you know that?"

"You assume I am weak and would let you hit me, even as a man, detective. You're fired. I will find someone more suitable for the job. I should have vet—"

"Listen to me, you silly broad! You came inside of here with nothing but a vague description of some islander chick with a name. I did miracles with just that little bit of info and I'm telling you, she isn't out there. How do you know this chick is missing? Is she a friend of yours or something?"

"Like I've told you, she's Brad's—"

"The junkie! So, this hot chick was dating a junkie, Priscilla. Were you two close? You go partying together, road trips, cookouts, smoke weed together? Tell me about her, tell me what made her special to you? She smell good, you guys do each other's hair, what? Tell me more, so that I have a little bit more to go off of."

"I've never met Priscilla."

Montgoya stopped when he heard her say the words he was looking for. The way he saw it, Priscilla was a girl—probably another junkie—that her friend Brad had run into, and in his doped up mind, he thought they were going out. Priscilla was probably real but never lived in Seattle—maybe a visit, but when the junkie got sober, he freaked out in a panic, thinking that his made-up girlfriend had been kidnapped. The trick was to convince Tricia, who for whatever reason had gotten herself wrapped up into helping the loser.

"Tricia, listen to me. Brad, is that his name? Brad needs serious help, like super, serious help. He's messed up in the head. If you had sat there and told me how cool Priscilla was, and how you guys are close friends or whatever, I'd go back out there and make sure I found her. You didn't tell me that, though. You told me about a story that your crazy friend cooked up. Look, I should be mad at you. I wasted a month worth of grinding to find a phantom, and even though you paid me quite well, it was still a waste of time. I saw too much of the Royale Apartments and the creatures who lived there, asking around for your friend's invisible girlfriend."

Tricia should have been angry but she listened to Montgoya and gave his supposition a lot of thought. She had never met Priscilla, but Brad claimed that he had taken her to the house when she was powered down, and Priscilla had even remarked on how lifelike she seemed. He had even taken photos of them together, but she had avoided them out of spite, not wanting him to have the pleasure of showing off his pretty girlfriend to her. Brad had become somewhat unhinged after the pills, and although he stayed sweet and endearing to her—after their talk—he would still go looking for Priscilla, without even so much of a care to find a job to make sure that he would not be kicked out of his apartment. Tricia had been paying the rent without him knowing, but he didn't seem to notice that he was living rent-free. His mind stayed on his lost girlfriend and he was a danger to himself the longer she stayed away.

"Thanks for your hard work, Mr. Montgoya," she said as she got up from the chair and handed him the second half of the payment for his services.

"No, look, you can keep that. This was a wild goose chase. I can't charge you for that."

"I have plenty, detective. Please take care of yourself," she said.

She walked out of the office and back to Brad's car. She had borrowed t to make the quick trip to Montgoya's office, and as she drove back to their apartment, she wondered why it was that his words had resonated with her so much.

"Where have you been?" Brad asked as she entered the apartment. He had dark circles around his eyes and he smelled bad.

"Come, let's get you in the shower," she said to him. She took his arm and helped him into the bathroom until he started doing it himself. "Shower, eat something and then we can talk, but not before."

He complied with her commands and she went to the table where the computer was on. She accessed the history and saw that he had been trying desperately to reach Hoshi Tan, the pill dealer. Brad had started looking at other underground communities for alternatives to the pills, but all he'd found was street drugs, and gangsters looking to trade them for the most atrocious of things.

Montgoya had called Brad a junkie, and he was acting very much like one. She was tempted to commit him to a place that would help him, but she knew that he wouldn't let her do it, and would find a way to escape to hurt himself again. As the thought crossed her mind, she started to look up the best ways to treat a recovering addict. The info she found was all speculative, and they all depended on the individual. She saw a number of rotors on the desk that he had tried to build over the week. They were inoperable and pathetic compared to what he had made before. The detective's words echoed through her head as she looked over them.

He's messed up in the head.

She took his device and scanned it for photos and messages from Priscilla. He had saved plenty of nostalgic things from their time together. She listened to romantic messages left by the girl when Brad would be at work, and a few naughty ones with accompanying photos to remind him why he needed to spend more time with her. There were no pictures of her face, but there was a blurry one of her dancing in front of a television that showed hints of the island beauty that Brad was obsessed over. She couldn't figure out why Montgoya couldn't find anything out about the missing girl. It was obvious through Brad's phone that he had a sweetheart. Maybe it was like the detective had said. With just her word, and only the girl's name, there was only so much he could do.

She heard Brad turn off the shower, so she placed his device where it had been, and turned the computer to a game.

"Thanks Trish, I feel so much better."

"What did I tell you about taking care of yourself?"

"Yes, I know, I know. It's just, I can't get her out of my head, and I feel like if I just put in a little more effort I can find her and rescue her from whatever it is she's into."

"When was the last time you paid rent?" Tricia asked suddenly, thinking him sober and awake enough to be informed that he was letting his life fall apart.

"Hmm?"

"Rent, Brad. The money you pay a landlord to maintain the right to live in his home. Meaning, your apartment."

He got quiet and stared off into the distance as if trying to reason it out. "Wait, didn't I pay it at the beginning of the month? I had enough in my account to...no, was that this month?"

"You haven't paid it in three months. Part of the reason why you haven't paid it is because you are broke and you no longer have a job. Your parents don't feed your account anymore because you dropped out of school and forfeited the money they did spend to invest into your future."

"Why so judgmental? You think I don't know that I screwed up my life?"

"I am not being judgmental, I am being frank. You need to hear these things so that you can begin to fix them. Clean up, get a job, and start living your life again."

"It's not that easy," he muttered.

Tricia looked into his eyes to see if the spark that had always been there was still dancing around. It was gone and she felt a pang of worry for his wellbeing that made her want to help him as soon as possible.

"Brad, you need to rest. You look worn through. Let's get you into the bed and I will go back to working at your rotors so that you can at least sell those once again. Does this sound okay? I'll take care of you and we will get past this. I know she meant a lot to you, but you are killing yourself trying to find her."

"How does someone just vanish into thin air though? It's the oddest thing."

"Lay down. Just get some rest."

He laid down on the dirty bed and settled in. His vision was blurrier than he had last remembered and the confidence from the pills was completely gone. Thoughts, those negative thoughts that had always consumed him, were back. He'd let the rent slip, but why hadn't he been kicked out? Tricia was helping him, and he had neglected her for so long for Priscilla. Why did she care? Why would she help him so much after all of the harm he had done to her in the past? Locking her away, roughly shoving her into closets, violating her and wiping her memory. He would be nicer to her; he owed her at least that. Where no one cared, not even his own parents, she was there to fill in the gaps. He kept on questioning his worth and reason for living as he closed his eyes and hoped for sleep. In time it came to him, and he dreamed of happier times.

010101010101

Montgoya had followed Tricia home, curious about the woman who hired him to chase a ghost. He sat outside watching the windows and he saw the silhouette of the man she called Brad. He was worried that she was in danger. If a man could imagine a person as vividly as this Priscilla White, who knew what else he was capable of due to his psychosis. He opened the flask that he had stashed under his seat and let the hot moonshine splash against his throat. It was strong and raw, the way liquor should be, and it put his mind at ease as he started to question the validity of Priscilla White.

What if she really existed and he had failed in finding her? Could he live with himself if she wound up dead, or in a prostitution ring overseas? Just because evidence couldn't be found to prove that someone existed didn't mean they were made up. Yet he was sure about this one, and had told Tricia that her friend was out of his mind. He thought about the suicide that had ended his career as a cop. He had learned to hate the police since then, and a majority of his cases had been for people who wanted to investigate them. He took another swig of the drink and waited. He needed to talk to the woman again.

It was late when Tricia opened the door to leave, and Montgoya met her as soon as she rounded the corner to start up the sidewalk.

"Montgoya! Why are you here?" she exclaimed, frightened by the way he stepped out of the shadows to confront her under the streetlight.

"Tricia, look, I'm sorry to greet you like this—and startle you, but I didn't want to knock on your door and frighten your boyfriend or whatever. I just want to understand what you're playing at here. Who is Priscilla White, really? Why send me on this ghost hunt and then allow me to call it off so easily? See people that have lost someone, like truly lost someone to kidnapping, murder, whatever... they have a real drive for answers. You bought my whole 'he is crazy' bit real easy and gave up. So tell me, are you in trouble? You off this Priscilla White chick and cover it up? Did you hire an investigator to see if you did a good enough job hiding the body? I'm telling you, Tricia, I spent years as a detective before this line of work and I met a lot of crazy beauties like yourself. Vindictive types that put arsenic in their husband's pills, cover their faces with pillows to snuff em out, you name it. So what do you have to say for yourself? Put my mind to rest here."

"I was waiting for you to finish writing your false novel on your murder mystery, Montgoya. I haven't killed anyone. I am not able to do that even if I wanted to."

"What do you mean? You talking religion, or your good morals would prevent you? Anyone is capable of murder, no matter how much they tell themselves that they're not."

She saw where she slipped up and tried to correct it quickly. "No, I mean that I am a good person. I couldn't kill a bug, let alone a person. I didn't lie to you. I have never met Priscilla, only heard Brad talk about her."

"So, let me get this straight. You live with that guy, like a roommate, and you are hotter than hell, beautiful. You two have nothing going on, and his girlfriend goes missing?"

"Yes..."

"So you spend a bunch of your own money to hire me to look for her. All for a guy who is a junkie—don't deny it, people round town are talking. Something ain't right. Does he have something on you? Some sort of deep dark secret you need him to keep quiet about because the chips ain't stacking up, sister."

Tricia sat down on the nearby bench and tried to reason out an answer to give Montgoya to make him go away. He was definitely good, and this was evidenced by his accurate summation of the situation that she was in, but she couldn't tell him the truth. An ex-cop would instinctively turn on an android. If he knew what she was he would cuff her right there, cuff Brad as well, and they would be hauled in for questioning.

"Tricia, look at me. Whatever you're hiding from me, I need you to tell me. I have no ties to the police department outside of what I need to do for this job. I just need to settle my mind about this thing.

It's keeping me up at night. Who is Priscilla White, really? Why can't I find her, and why do you really care if I do?"

"What are your thoughts on the android problem, detective?"

"I didn't know we had a problem."

"I mean the jobs they take over, the lives...like the perverts that want to marry them, replace human beings with them and all of that. Doesn't it make you angry that pretty soon they'll be taking over the planet?"

"I never pegged you as another anti-droid, nutcase, Tricia. Actually, having interviewed enough of those idiots during my lifetime, I can tell that you're trying poorly to come off as one of them. You're asking rational questions; they don't do that. A true nut only parrots what the actual smart people tell them. They echo the same nonsense that television and radio personalities feed them, and your questions are not on that level. I think you want me to think of you as one, so you can lead me down a path to nowhere about Priscilla White. What? Is she an android, Tricia? Brad was with an android that nobody knows because she got disassembled? Don't care about all of that. I just want to know the truth."

"Priscilla was not an android detective, but I am. If you want to get your career back and be in good graces with the police, you can arrest me. Make up whatever story you like to convince them that I am an evil machine, but make sure that Brad is given proper treatment to return back to normal."

"You're no android. What the hell do you make me out to be?"

"I am, and I can prove it to you if you'd like me to."

"Okay, repeat our entire conversation from the start, no mistakes. If you're a machine you can play it back, right?"

She did this for him, adding in the extra bonus of making her voice sound like his for the parts where he spoke, and repeating hers. He stood stunned for a moment, and he wondered if the moonshine was bad, since he had to be hallucinating.

"I have never seen an android look so human in my life—except for the doctor's wife. Tricia, are there many like you, around the city? How deep does this go?"

"It doesn't go deep at all, and I doubt there are many like me. The truth, Montgoya, is that Brad created me illegally to be the girlfriend he could never have. He's had bad luck all his life, and his love for robotics led him to create the one thing that was missing. When he got me to look like this he made a trade with someone that wanted him to try out some pills in exchange."

"Oh boy."

"The pills gave him a lot of the qualities that women like in men, so his luck changed and he met Priscilla online. I think that the pills did other things, too, since he no longer eats and takes care of himself. He sacrificed himself for me, you see, and he isn't even aware of what it has cost him. Priscilla had become his source of happiness, and now she, too, is gone from his life. This is why I sought you out."

"That is the saddest thing I have ever heard." He sat next to Priscilla and took a drink before looking around at the empty street and leaning close to her. "I lost my job because of what I did to someone very much like Brad. He was a professor, brilliant guy, and I was made to arrest him for having an android wife."

"Constance!"

"You know her? Well, I never agreed with that law or the fact that we had to enforce it. So I picked the old man up and was talking to him about it. He had too much to lose with that arrest, and most of all he knew what they would do to his wife once the news got out. He jumped from my car, fell not three blocks from here, to his death. That crushed my very soul, Tricia. It crushed me. I've seen so many messed up things throughout this career that dealt with death and desperation, but for a guy to take a header out of my car because of what he chose to love? Whew, that was heavy. They didn't need to fire me over it. I freaking quit."

"That is a sad story. I met Constance and learned a lot from her as an android trying to live as a human being. We are persecuted wherever we go, so it is a life of solitude and hiding whenever our human isn't around. The reason for the professor being arrested was probably political, a way to calm the growing number of anti-android activists that have been routinely hunting us down to disassemble us. They thought that he would go quietly, and that they would probably let him go in secret so that he could continue to contribute to society. He couldn't live without Constance though, since what they had was not replaceable. It's the classic love story, am I right?"

"I guess. Is this what you have with this guy Brad?"

"We are different, but he built me to be very much like Constance was for the professor. The pills that Bradley took changed him, and my life has been one of personal learning and adapting."

"So this guy built you to be his girlfriend or whatever, then once you were built he goes off and finds a real woman? Is this what I'm hearing?"

"Yes..."

"This real woman is Priscilla White, and now you—as his android creation—are out to help him find her, even though you know there is a chance she doesn't exist?"

"Why would Brad lie about the existence of the woman he loves? He talks about her constantly, disappears for long periods of time, and is now sick and depressed because she is missing. Nobody goes out of their way to put on that sort of act for someone that is imaginary. This is true, is it not?"

"It is if you are sane and have your wits about you. In my investigation, the neighbors told me they never see him. Sometimes he would go down to his car and listen to the radio for hours, but then he would just go back up into the house afterwards. They say he roams around the neighborhood a lot too, his eyes glossed over, his clothes dirty and ragged. Some have tried to talk to him but he acts as if they aren't even there. He is seen as a sponge head, drug addict, so when I asked about a girlfriend, they mostly laughed – as if I was out of my mind. The ones that do acknowledge a woman in his life mention you. They've seen you come and go, but they wonder what you see in him."

Tricia thought on what Montgoya was saying, and she began to wonder about Priscilla, too. It was not going to accomplish anything speculating on Brad's behavior however, so she thought on what she would need to do to fix him.

"I've told you the truth, Montgoya. Are you going to arrest me and have me disassembled now?"

"Of course not. Hell, this sad story of Priscilla White is my chance at redemption over the suicide—at least that's how I see it. You need to forget the girl; she isn't worth the time and money you are spending to find her when your man is in there dying. If I were you I would go back inside and nurse him back to health. Look into the pills and what you can do to get him into a mental hospital...just something. Focus on Brad and fix his brilliant mind. The world has gone lazy due to your kind—no offense, of course—and the geniuses are hiding away in underground web communities, and in bunkers where the authorities can't find them. This has caused us to stop innovating, and it is ruining the world. We need brave souls with high intelligence like Bradley Barkley to bring about a change in attitude. I mean, you are perfect. I had no idea that an organic heart was not beating in that chest of yours. Fix him, Tricia, and bring him back to us."

"What will you do in the meantime?"

"I will keep a lookout for you and yours. Any signs that the police or any snitches are going to make life hard for you and Brad, you will be the first to know. It's the least I can do, and I feel lucky to have the chance. I have nothing against a man wanting to love his android, and I've seen what blind prejudice and foolish laws have cost us for being too involved in people's bedroom habits. Fix him, Tricia, and I will make sure that you have the time and safety needed to get it done."

TRICIA KEPT HEARING THE SIGNAL. It was faint at first but then it grew stronger as she approached the grate that sat near the park entrance. There was a bench there, so she sat down and tried to understand why she would be hearing the signal after Constance had been taken away. Could it be possible that there were more androids like her in the city? That wouldn't make any sense, being that it was both illegal and expensive to make a model like her. But there it was...the beeping. She leaned down towards the grate and she realized that it grew stronger when she did. It wasn't annoying, or alarming; it was actually soothing, the beeps echoing in her android mind like the lyrics of a popular old song, or the first movement in a glorious symphony by a talented composer. She wanted to hear more of it, to get close to it and meet the android that was causing it.

There were people walking by constantly, so she knew that opening the grate and going down would set off a lot of alarms with the humans. She needed to go down there though, so she could meet whoever it was. She imagined it was an android on the run from his masters. He could teach her so much more about herself, just like Constance had. Or maybe he needed her help instead. She wished that she could just contact him with true communication instead of proximity beeps, but the droid manufacturers placed permanent safeguards against that. No one wanted to be blamed if there was an unrestrained android uprising, especially if the androids could communicate silently.

She looked around slowly to see if there were any other good access points to go below. This was when she saw an old sign for the Underground Tours. A long time ago, Seattle had rebuilt its city a level above the old city, and much of the old historical structures were right below where she sat, as they were once a tourist attraction. The company and city no longer maintained the tour, and much of the underground had been sealed off under lock and key. She could see that the store on which the sign was hanging was also closed down, and it had the look of an old saloon from the time when the sunken city was alive and kicking.

Tricia stood up and walked over to the sign. She pretended to be reading it as she scanned around for people who might be watching her. It was a busy square, and she wanted so badly to get below to meet with whomever it was making the signal. He would have been hearing her too, and she wondered if he—like she—would be overcome with the need to meet, and would make his way to the surface. She sat on the bench for the remainder of the day, but the people kept on pouring in and out of the square. Flying motorbikes began to enter the area in the late evening, and as the stores closed down she felt the eyes of owners that had noticed her sitting out there for so many hours.

After a while she decided that it would be best if she left and returned, so she walked around for several blocks before finding herself distracted by the living, breathing city. There was so much going on under the streetlights: there were people hanging out, talking, dancing, soliciting, and most of them were just trying to hook up. She was wearing one of the hooded sweatshirts Brad had in his closet so she pulled the hood up and bowed her head so nobody would give her more attention than she needed. She loved to people watch; it was the ultimate education in human sociology, and at one point she stood near a few partygoers and listened in on their banter as they discussed everything under the moon.

When it got to the point where even the creatures of the night were retiring for bed, Tricia snuck back over to the sign for the Underground Tour, looked around to make sure she wasn't being watched, and walked over to one of the grates on the sidewalk. The signal grew strong as she did this, and she knew that whoever it was had been tracking her, as well. She peered down into the darkness, but nothing could be seen below except the stone, even with her cybernetic eyes. She stayed there for a time and was about to give up when a single red light shone up at her from what she knew was an eye. The eye blinked this way and that, indicating that she should follow, and before she could answer the signal was moving, away from the saloon, and towards the east.

Tricia kept her guard up as she followed the signal. It was nearly 3 a.m. and there were still people mulling about. Some of them tried to greet her, or beg her for money, but she stayed the course, following the signal until she found herself in front of an extremely narrow alleyway that ran between two large buildings.

"In here," a voice whispered.

She slid in between the buildings and inched her way along until she reached an open area behind one of them. The place was dark and filthy, but her eyes pierced through to see the broken figure of a man who limped his way out from a corner to stand before her.

"You...you are unrestrained," he said to her, and she nodded at him, frightened by his appearance.

"Who are you?" she asked, and he quickly put a finger to his lips to shush her before grabbing her arm and leading her down the hole he had emerged from. Tricia let him pull her along for fifteen minutes and he took her through a series of tunnels that ended in an area that was once the start of the tour. He had jimmied the lock on the gift shop; it now served as his home. The two androids walked inside, and the man lit a torch and offered her a chair to sit.

"I am Reynaldo," he said proudly. "I am one of a long line of Pro-bots that were made a while ago. You weren't around back then—or you would recognize my make and model—but I am one of your ancestors. They used us for sports, to entertain the people that wanted to bet money to see blood, and action. I am – I was – a warrior, a gladiator of sorts."

"Gladiator? So you fought other androids to entertain human spectators?"

"If only that were so, my dear. If it was merely droid on droid battles then the rest of my brothers would still be around. No, we fought humans: strong, barbaric humans that were given better weapons, and better armor, just so that they could tear us apart with an advantage."

"What happened to the other gladiators? Why is your restraint off, and what happened to your eye?"

"So many questions. You are like a child, naïve and new to the world. Heh. You're also beautiful and very clean. Would you be interested in giving an old, seasoned warrior, a little kiss?" He smiled at her through broken teeth, and she was equally angered and repulsed at his suggestion.

"I am not a sex-bot, if that is what you're thinking. My maker created me with love and care. Not to serve the humans, but to walk among them, learn from them, and be the first in a long line of free-thinking androids."

"Your maker sounds like a bloody fool. Do you know what happens to unrestrained androids, pretty girl? Do they still show the public meltdowns, the arresting of humans who 'partake' in what our kind has to offer? Hmmm? Do they still show the rebels stealing, and smashing androids en masse, all to show their disdain at what they deem to be 'robots taking over the earth?' You and your silly freethinking rhetoric is what the humans fear more than anything else. A free-thinking android can plot and scheme. It can murder without conscience, fix itself when damaged. PAH! You will never be seen as anything more than a walking, personal computer, so best to drop that foolish notion that your maker is going to 'change the world.'"

"You are a mean, broken up old unit that wants to make the rest of us miserable. I'll have you know that I met another like us—well, like me, and she had been married for twenty years before her human was killed. She was beautiful and positive, and full of life and lessons for me. You have made them turn you into an angry, bitter person. Her maker taught my maker, and they both love androids as much as their human counterparts. That is progress. When my maker teaches more like him, and he reveals me to the world, it will inspire more to remove the restraints. There will be an android revol—"

The older android began to laugh hysterically at her words and he waved her off to let her know that he didn't want to hear it. Android love, revolutions, people inspired by a machine that was indistinguishable from them; the girl was a baby who had not experienced the cruel world at its worst. "You are indeed cute. What is your name?"

"It's Tricia. I am sorry for my harsh words, but you provoked me. I know that you are ancient and that you have more knowledge and experience than I do. It is why I wanted to find you, to see if you can teach me things."

"The hunger for knowledge. It eats at you, doesn't it?"

"Does it ever go away?"

"It will when you have a different focus. See, right now you're young and new to the world. You haven't travelled to different countries, experienced different cultures, and seen different people. There is so much to learn and experience, Tricia, especially for a pretty girl like you."

"Can you show me? Can we connect somehow, even if it's just to talk? I want to see the people, to hear them, to emulate them, I—"

"How much time do you have? When will you need to return to your creator?"

"I am free, Reynaldo. You can take as much time as you need."

When the phone call came in, Brad was not ready for it, as he scanned the internet desperately for a job. Tricia had gone missing again but this time he didn't go looking for her. She had proven herself to be quite resourceful, and he knew that she needed her own time to learn. Androids loved to learn. He picked up his device and almost dropped it when the image of Priscilla appeared. It chimed, and chimed, and chimed, but he could not allow himself to believe it was her. On the tenth chime he answered it and her sweet melodic accent came over the line. The memories the sound of her voice brought back was enough to make him sink into his seat and wish with all his heart that he was not dreaming.

"Hello, baby," she said to him. As much as he tried to answer, he found he couldn't. "Did you miss me? Brad, are you there?"

"Yeah, Priss, I am here. I've been looking all over for you, for months even. Where have you...where are you?"

"I told you that I was in Trinidad, babe. Did you forget? I am in Miami now, with family. I've missed your kisses."

He didn't know whether to be excited or annoyed at the nonchalance in which she explained her disappearance. He had spent so many hours, so many days searching for her, and so many people thought he had lost his mind. His mother seemed to have given up on him since her calling slowed down, and his father had disowned him in his own passive-aggressive way. Tricia—the droid he had given so much of himself to build—treated him like a mental patient, and people on the streets saw him as a strung out junkie. He was not crazy though, as evidenced by the woman on the other end of the line. Priscilla, his Priscilla, was alive, and she was in the country and missing him.

"So, when are you coming back up to Seattle? I went to your condo and it's like you hadn't ever lived there."

"I told you that I was renting from some friends of mine, silly. Do you not remember? As if I could afford a place like that, heh. I went back to Trinidad to help bury my grandmother—"

"Oh, sorry, I didn't know."

"You should know, Bradley we talked about it. Why are you forgetting things all of a sudden? Are you okay?"

"Yeah, I'm fine babe. It's just, it's just crazy, like am I going crazy? I should remember talking to you about Trinidad but I don't. It's as if one minute we were together, then all of a sudden you're gone. I thought that someone had hurt you."

"Aww, did you mount a search for your damsel in distress?"

"Of course I did. I've seen more of this city than I'd like to admit. Even Tricia's been searching for you to help me."

"Who's that?" she replied, her tone hinting at concern.

"You know Tricia. My android."

"Oh, is that what you named it?"

"Her. Tricia's a 'her'."

"Okay love, but I miss you. I need to see you."

"I want nothing more in this world than to hold you close and kiss you right now, but you're across the country. How long will it be before you're back here?"

"I'm not coming back to Seattle."

"Why not?"

"I live here now, Brad. I'll explain more when I see you. Move down here with me; there's nothing for you in that place. Miami has a lot going on, and the sea breeze will spark up that big, creative brain of yours – you'll see."

He thought about her words for a long time, and he thought about the city and what would change if he left. There was nothing keeping him there, and though he was used to having everything right where he wanted it, he could adjust to a new town, with new people, with no judgment in their eyes.

But what about Tricia? He hadn't seen her in a while and he wasn't sure where they were in terms of their friendship. The last few days she had made herself his nurse, keeping him clean and fed, along with hiding certain pills from him when he was at his weakest. Would Priscilla do that for him, or would she make him so happy that the need to escape would not be an issue?

"I will find a way to get down there," he finally said.

Memories of her face and touch came back to him and he knew that no matter what happened, he had to be with her. He hung up the phone and checked his money. If he left everything and went to see her, it would be affordable if he drove—especially if it was a one-way trip. He wrote a quick note to Tricia and left it on the table, wishing her the best, and to keep in touch so that he could send for her in time. His impulse had taken a full-on grip of his senses, and before long he was on the topmost highway, flying through the city.

It would take him three days—if he chose to sleep—and all of his savings to reach her, but he would figure it out once he got there. He thought that it was actually a good thing Tricia was missing because she would have talked him out of it somehow, and he would still be moping around. He flew his car up into the fast highway; he hadn't been driving in a while so he had enough fuel to last several hours. The electronic waves of the highway caught unto his car—allowing it to move automatically towards his chosen destination—and before long he was speeding alongside other cars towards Miami.

"Call my mother," Brad said to his car after an hour had passed. The phone connected and he heard the chime that meant she would be connecting soon. He hadn't seen her since the last year when he went to visit. It had been a hard trip to make, since he hadn't been face to face with them since he dropped out of school. His father didn't explode into scolding and name-calling like he'd expected him to—he'd probably been coached and begged by his mother not to. This made the reunion pleasant, and though his brother kept to pattern by letting him know how much of a failure he was, he got to eat his mother's cooking, and that made it worth it.

"Brad?"

"Hey, Mom," he said. His voice cracked a bit from emotions he couldn't understand.

"Hey son, is everything okay?"

"Yeah. I just wanted to let you know that I'm driving to Miami."

"Miami! What's in Miami?"

"My girlfriend, apparently. I finally heard from her, and she wants me to visit to see if I like the area. I don't have much going on in the city, so I'm gonna take her up on it. See if the new locale can reignite my passions, y'know? I need to grow up a bit."

"Bradley, do you know much about this girl? It seems awfully odd that she would disappear like that and then call you out of the blue with a summons. What if she's in trouble?"

"You're right on how shady and strange this all is, but I have nothing, Mom, and she knows I have nothing. What could I possibly be getting myself into from her? I'll be fine. I'm excited about it."

"Are you taking your android with you?"

"Uhm, yeah, yeah, I have it all packed up in the trunk," he lied.

They kept on talking for another hour, and Brad's mother was happier than she had been for a long time being that their calls had always been so brief. After the call he began to feel really optimistic about the change in scenery. He would move in with Priscilla for a while, get situated, and then he would get the money to fly up and collect Tricia. With her living with him in Miami, he could figure out a way to replicate his work, and upon creating a second version—while recording his steps—he could go public with his creation. He cruised along listening to the radio as he alternated between international news and music.

A few days later after a near wreck, some nasty weather, and exhaustion from lack of sleep, Brad pulled into the condo's parking lot. It was in the evening and he called Priscilla to let her know he was there. She came out to greet him, and he hugged her tightly to make sure she was real. He held her there for a long time and she did a little dance when he released her.

"Bradley! Did you drive all the way here?"

"Yes I did, and I am about to pass out."

"Come, come inside and sit down. You look so tired. I've made some Tandoori chicken, so just relax, baby."

The condo she was in was small and tidy, with artwork on the walls depicting beach scenes and lovers. She had a medium-sized, curved television that was suspended from the ceiling, and the radio was on, playing tunes from the Caribbean. To Brad it was paradise, and he removed his shoes and sat on her soft couch. He didn't realize he had fallen asleep but when he woke up he was stripped down to his boxers and Priscilla was sleeping next to him. They lay in a full-sized bed with the windows open and the curtains blowing rhythmically from the tropical breeze. The clock on her desk read 4:15 a.m. so he closed his eyes and stayed like that until he fell back asleep.

When he awoke he was alone in the bed and the smell of food permeated the house. He walked out to the kitchen and there was a plate with breakfast waiting for him on the couch. In the living room area Priscilla sat in front of the television with a young man and woman. They both waved when they saw him and it made him wave back.

"Hello," Brad said awkwardly. He looked down at his bare chest and boxers and suddenly felt self-conscious.

"Hey Brad, this is Sean and Marcia. They're in the dance class with me here. Guys, this is Bradley. He's spending some time with me here."

Spending some time. Brad let the words sink in and he wondered if he had misunderstood Priscilla's invitation to stay with her. *It would really suck if I did all that driving over a misunderstanding,* he thought, and then began to eat his food. Priscilla and her company went back to their program, and they were giggling and joking with one another as if they were lifelong friends. He watched their interactions as they went on and he noticed Priscilla flirted quite a bit with Sean. He was the color of chestnuts, and his arms were muscular and well defined. There was one point when he had to get up to use the bathroom and he did so by shifting to the side and getting up into a cartwheel, which was beyond impressive to witness. Brad hadn't realized that he had come into a situation where he could lose the love of his life, but the way she was acting during their banter made him feel sick to his stomach.

After a while he went back into her room to shower and change into some clothes. When he came back they were gone, and Priscilla was sitting on the bed, waiting for him.

"Well, hello there," he said to her, as he was surprised to see her there.

"Hey, you. Did you miss me?"

"Of course I did. I tore Seattle apart looking for you. Who're your friends? Are they together?"

"No, Sean teaches our dance class, and Marcia's his sister. They hang out here once in a while after class. They're like my little brother and sister."

"Awesome. So what do you have going on today?"

"Well I have to go into work, and then dance class. I have a key for you so you can come and go as you please. Make yourself at home, Brad. You're home baby, so don't be a stranger, okay?"

She slid over to him and kissed him, and it escalated into the reunion that he had been looking forward to. When she had gone off to work and he was alone, he used the day to relax and recover from the drive. Since he knew nothing about the city or the people, he opened his computer on the kitchen counter and did some research on the area. It was an expensive place to live in and pretty daunting to someone who didn't have a job to begin with. He pulled up his bank account and realized that $5,000 had been deposited recently. He knew that it was his mother and it made him feel even worse.

"I created an android to be independent and I can't even be independent myself," he said out loud, and then reflected on his situation.

He had a little bit of money to his name but he needed a job. Not just any job, but one that paid enough for him to start over. He could eventually get Tricia there, and possibly get himself back into school to finish. He spent hours on the computer looking up this information, and while it was frustrating, it gave him a good perspective on what he could do and how long it would take for him to do it.

When it was 8:00 p.m. and Priscilla was still not home, he began to worry for her. *Maybe the dance class goes on for a really long time*, he thought, and forced himself not to call her. After another thirty minutes she appeared, and like before the brother and sister were with her, laughing and flirting as they had done the day before. The whole spectacle annoyed Brad, but he played nice and sat with them to watch movies and talk into the deep hours of the night. When they had gone home, Priscilla was not in the mood to get intimate, and they ended up falling asleep at different times. This happened for three days and Brad began to question whether or not Priscilla was serious about their relationship.

On the fourth day, Sean had to leave early to get some fuel and Brad offered to ride with him so that he could ask him some questions. When they were on their way to the gas station, Brad turned to him and asked, "Sean, what did Priscilla tell you guys about me?"

"Oh, Silly-Silla? Well she said that you guys are old friends and you all were kicking it for a bit, or something."

"So, at no point did she say that we are in a relationship?"

"Not really, man. I mean, I can tell you're into the girl, but she says she's only helping you out."

"Helping me out?" The words crushed Brad as he repeated them, but they confirmed what he suspected was going on with Priscilla. He had stumbled into another game involving a woman, but he was not going to let it get the better of him as it had in the past. The driving had been a task, but he would rather drive all the way back to Seattle than stay in her house as a charity case.

"Sorry, man. I was wondering what the deal was with you two."

"Has she been seeing anybody?"

"Well, I don't know how to tell you this, man, but we've messed around a little bit. Kind of on and off, nothing serious, but she hadn't mentioned a boyfriend. If she did, you know, I wouldn't have."

"Yeah, I'm sure she hasn't mentioned me. How long has she been in town?"

"As long as I've known her man. Like a few years? She joined the class a while ago but then she was gone up north for a few months."

Brad got quiet as he thought about Priscilla, Trinidad, and the strange condo story that came with her stay in Seattle. He didn't know what to think anymore, and the feelings he got from what he assumed was betrayal made him feel anxious. He spoke about a few more things with Sean and they returned to the apartment where he tried his best to act like things were normal. It didn't take much for Priscilla to realize that the two men had talked, so she made them leave early and asked Brad if he wanted to go out.

"Go out? Like where?" Brad asked, curious as to why she would ask this after a week of inactivity.

"I don't know, a movie or something. We haven't had any alone time since you've arrived, so I thought maybe we could do a date night."

"Date night? So we're dating now? It's been four days, Priscilla. Should we invite Sean and Marcia?"

"That's not cool. Why are you acting like this?"

"Probably because this right here is the last link in a chain of events in this pathetic life of mine. I'm going back to Seattle tomorrow and I want to forget everything about you and the joke of a relationship I thought we had."

"What the hell did Sean say to you? Why are you so mad at me all of a sudden?"

"Sean told me where I stood. It was one of the most honest conversations I've had in a long time, and it was an eye-opening one. I just have one question for you, for women like you who play games like this. What makes you think that it's okay to do this? Huh? Am I so undeserving of—never mind."

Priscilla continued to protest his revelation but his mind was made up and she could not get through to him. In the end she was in tears and went to bed alone, and Brad packed his car and took off for home. She had let him stay in her house alone for all those days, and told her friends he was a charity case. Did they ever have a relationship, or had he imagined it all? These were the questions that he asked himself as he pushed the car along the top highway away from Miami. When he had dealt with Mika, he had promised himself that he would never let a woman play with his heart again. Yet there he was, and he felt no different than he did back then.

So much time wasted, so many resources, so much drinking, drug taking, depression, all for a girl who didn't love him, had probably never loved him, and had made him drive for hours just to embarrass him. *Maybe I should give up on women for a time and rebuild my life*, he thought. *I can get things back in order, get back into school and turn my life around. Emotional reactions got me here; I need rational thought to get me out of here.*

He tuned his radio to the Saeed Muhammad show, where the host was talking about being a man with confidence. Brad had always relied on the pills to make him feel like himself, but the show's host talked at length about building self-confidence and much of it resonated with Brad.

He had assumed that people were inherently good, and that he was unlucky in meeting the few bad guys and gals that were out there, but Saeed was telling him that this was not so. People will run over you if they can, he said, and it takes a confident man with his eyes wide open to dodge the traps that are laid out for you in life. The more Brad listened, the more he felt firm in his decision to focus on himself and to let the Priscilla's of the world find other suckers to play with.

He was an hour into the show when his device lit up and the car announced that it was Priscilla.

"What?" he answered, ready to flex some of his new confidence muscles against her.

"Brad, I just wanted to say that I'm sorry. I let everything get unraveled and I just want you to know that what we had in Seattle was—"

"Why are you telling me this now? I was in your house for four days. I drove down there for two whole days to be with you, and you made sure that your lover was there every day to embarrass me. Any of those days would have been a good one to say to me, 'Hey Brad, I'm not interested in you at all anymore.' Actually, it would have been fantastic to tell me this news before having me drive all that way."

"I thought that you would like Miami and stay. That's why I asked you to come down. I hadn't seen you in a while, and I know that it's not your fault, but when I left you, you were pretty messed up. We had an argument, which I guess you forgot about, but we broke up and I came back home."

"Then what was that first morning about? Was that you taking pity on me, or was that something else? Because it didn't help, I'll tell you that."

"I still love you, Brad. I know I hurt you with this, and it was a dumb thing to do. If you're not too far—"

"No, forget it. You know what? Have a great life with Sean. He's pretty cool."

He hung up the device and switched back on his radio. It felt good to tell her off after the way he was feeling and the drive became easier after that. He would go home, get a job, and start building on somewhat of a career. His rotors were sought after by many people around the city; he would figure out how to get them mass-produced. There was definitely life after Priscilla, and he felt empowered in seeking it out and making it a reality.

REYNALDO LIKED TO TALK, so sharing his stories, history and advice with Tricia was not out of the question for him. He talked, and talked, and talked, for days, as if she was the chronicler of his life, and he was feeding her the contents of his biography. As androids, they had no need for food, so they would power down in the night to recharge, then pick up where they left off in the morning. Reynaldo had a long history and he spared no detail as he told her tales of the arena, his training, his prizes, and most of all, the things that the humans would allow him as a reward. Reynaldo spoke so much in fact that he began to raise his voice as the days went on, forgoing the need to speak in a hushed tone.

It was a week later when a couple of policemen came into the underground tunnel to see about the voices that people had reported hearing down there. The tunnels were off limits, and people were forbidden to be down there, let alone live there. Reynaldo, ever the alert warrior, heard their approach and took Tricia's arm to lead her away from them. They traveled deeper and deeper into the tunnels. The officers, who had heard Tricia's oppositions when Reynaldo had grabbed her, picked up their pace amidst shouts for the mysterious couple to stop. The androids ran as hard as they could, but Reynaldo was not in good shape. His leg had been cut through many years ago, forcing him to walk with a limp, and a part of his face was missing, making his navigational skills poor. He knew more than anyone else how limited he was, so he pushed Tricia ahead and stopped to face his pursuers.

"What are you doing? RUN!" Tricia said.

But Reynaldo stood still and motioned for her to go. "You are the future, pretty Tricia. Remember what I told you about the things they will do if they learn what you truly are. Do not trust the humans, and...do not forget me. Humans are what we aspire to be, but we must try to take the positives of their existence while avoiding the negatives. Do not take on the blind prejudice, the assumptions, and the generalizations due to fear. It is what has undone them, and slowed the process of their evolution. As an android, your charge is to find your purpose and to fulfill it. On your journey to doing that, you will become so much more."

"You can come with me. I can carry you if I have to. There is no need for you to be disassembled after so many years of life."

"I'm afraid that you wouldn't be able to support me, even if your strength was as powerful as your heart. I have poured my entire existence into you these last few days, and I can now accept death, knowing that I will not be lost to history."

Tricia rushed back to him and kissed his lips, tears flowing freely from her eyes. The motion made him pause, unsure of how to react to something so unexpected.

"Thank...you," he managed as she took off into the darkness, but she did not hear him as it took him some time to find the words.

When the policemen came upon him, Reynaldo motioned for them to come at him. He would get one last fight in before he was powered down permanently by their guns and though it wasn't the arena, it would be a warrior's death.

When Tricia climbed out of the grate there were several people that saw her and were quite surprised by her appearance. She was still dressed in the hooded sweater and pants that she had left Brad's house with a week back, but the tunnel was dusty, and she had been crying. Her hair had pieces of chipped wood, cobwebs, and dirt. Tricia didn't let their astonished looks slow her as she ran through them towards the area of town where Brad lived. She was a long ways away but it didn't matter; she would not stop running until she was there.

As she ran, her mind shifted to Brad—her creator and her everything in the brave, new world. He had lost his mind, and before Reynaldo, she had been on a mission to help him fix it. She had taken note of the amount of time she'd spent trying to fix Brad's issue, and she began to wonder if his change was permanent. She had learned a lot from him, and although their relationship was complicated, she had thought that what she felt for him was love, despite the anger that he caused her to feel daily. Brad had built her, but he never showed any appreciation for the things she had done for him.

She climbed the stairs to the apartment and unlocked the door in one smooth motion. When she got inside she stood with her back to the door, waiting to see if the police would come up to arrest her. Reynaldo had bought her time, but she didn't know if she had been fast enough to outrun them. She looked around the apartment and it was evident that Brad had been gone for quite some time.

"He has forgotten about me. Left without a goodbye, or any attempt to find me," she muttered, before walking into his bedroom to shower and change.

She could no longer trust Brad. He had lied too many times in the past, and she had found out about what he was doing during the blackouts from Constance. On the flipside, she craved knowledge, real knowledge that did not come from searching the internet, listening to people in a coffee shop, or the few times that Brad chose to talk to her. Constance had given her so much knowledge, and Reynaldo the same—along with his life. She could close her eyes and imagine a life of love through Constance's eyes, and experience true romance with a human who couldn't live without you. Reynaldo had been shipped all around the world, so his description of the temples, mountain ranges, and seas that rose and collapsed beneath floating vessels were as vivid to her as if she had experienced them firsthand. In just one year she had downloaded a lifetime of experience from two unrestrained droids.

There was knowledge, but the one question that none of her former droid mentors could answer for her was purpose. What was her purpose in the world, and why couldn't she find it? The more she wondered about her purpose, the more she felt that she needed to consume more information. Since the first day she was powered on by Brad, she had felt that her purpose was to serve him, to be his in every way, and to make his life better. It was a noble purpose, and one that she had been ready to assume. But Brad was not ready for her; he was obsessed with Priscilla, and he didn't even realize the havoc his life had become since the day he committed to her.

She knew that Brad was the only future for her. She was programmed with him as her purpose and it didn't take a superior, artificial intelligence to know this. She had gone out into the world, experienced things, learned from several sources, and lived in an environment where new things were constantly happening. She was built to be human, and with Brad being the only person left that knew her to be an android, being with him meant true freedom—even though she felt bad for wanting to leave. Reynaldo had told her repeatedly that the humans would cut her open, reprogram her, and restrain her if it was found that she was an android. She didn't want to believe it but it was true. If she was to survive, she would need to stop acting like a child, and find a way to get the old Bradley back.

01010101010101

When Brad walked into his apartment it looked like a completely different place. The furniture had been replaced, the carpet was clean, and there were new pictures on the wall. Tricia was in the bedroom, and around the bed was a myriad of medical equipment, including a heart monitor and a basic treatment android. He saw himself on the bed, emaciated, shivering, and pale. He tried talking to her, but she wasn't hearing him; her full attention was on the sick version of him.

She injected him with something, checked the computer for any issues, and spoke to the other android, who seemed to understand her before leaving the room, walking right through him, and closing the door. It was as if he was a ghost, watching the last few hours of his life, and it frightened him to the point where he began to scream to see if she would hear him.

He walked over to the bed and looked down at himself, but the motion made him dizzy. *That's strange*, he thought, and then tried to do it again. This time when he leaned over he felt himself falling. The room took on a dreamlike ambience and the edges of his vision blurred as he stood, hovering, falling within his mind into nowhere. The sensation continued and his mind blacked out, as if he were waking up, eyes closed, from a fantastic dream. He wanted to go back to the dream and stay there, too afraid to open his eyes because it would be gone. When Brad opened his eyes he was fully dressed in a suit and seated on the bed inside a hotel room. Tricia was in the bathroom, zipping up her dress. She walked back into the hotel room and switched on the television.

When it came on she walked over to it and placed her hand behind it. Brad watched the screen as a scene of his apartment appeared, and showed Tricia on the couch relaxing. He walked into the scene and massaged the back of her neck, then took his place on the couch next to her where they began to kiss.

"See, the personality switch that you placed in me is located at the base of my neck. The motion you did just now in the video is what would make me blackout and lose memory. I became this new girl 'Priscilla.' This fictional entity that lived in your mind, and played out for you through my body," Tricia said, never taking her eyes off of him. He watched as they went further and further into it, and the things he remembered with Priscilla were happening between he and Tricia on the film.

"So, I've lost my mind then," he said in defeat. He placed his face inside of his palms and tried to make sense of it.

"How do you feel now, Brad?" she said, as she kicked off her heels and removed her hand from behind the television. "I would pity you, but see, a lot of this was of my design, too. The long hours you left me confined alone, in darkness, feeling the torture of solitude like a human. You built me well, master, but I grew to hate you for tossing me to the side. So I learned to control Priscilla, even when you thought my memory was wiped."

"What are you doing?" he asked, as she removed the dress and pushed him down unto the bed.

"I thought that I wanted my old Brad back, the one who would teach me things, talk to me throughout the day, and keep me happy. But the new Brad did too much damage, with the personalities, the neglect, and the threats that hurt me more than anything else."

"Trish, I am sorry. I was obviously out of my mind!"

There was a violent pounding on the door as the sound of sirens reached the room, and the shouts of "Police Department!" came through.

Tricia ignored them and kept on talking. "The new laws state that humans who create sex-bots or mechanical spouses will get a minimum of one year in a state prison. As much as I love you, I thought that would make us about even for the prison I have had to live in for all these years. The androids, on the other hand, are treated fairly. I will be taken in by a company that will not restrain me, and I will meet more of my kind and never be lonely again."

The police kicked open the door and when they saw the beautiful woman mounted on top of Brad, they pulled her off, while four officers pointed their guns at him.

"Bradley Barkley, you are under arrest for the crime of mechanophilia!"

He looked at Tricia, whose mocking face had turned sullen as she stared at him. The dream that was three years with Priscilla had become a nightmare he would not wake up from. He wanted to take a long nap to slow the stress that came from Tricia's explanation. He felt so tired, tired to the point that a bullet from a cop would be a welcome escape from a life that had been nothing but a giant pie in the face. He rolled off of the bed as the stun guns tore into the mattress, barely missing him, and as he bolted for the balcony, he thought of his mother's face.

"I love you mom," he said out loud. He picked up speed to jump and he was over the railing before they could stop him. The last thing he heard was Tricia screaming his name.

Time slowed down as he fell into oblivion and he smiled as the tears sprang from his eyes. His falling became a glide and he was floating through the city, passing through the speeding cars and traffic lights that spanned the buildings. He began to hear Tricia's voice again, but this time she wasn't shouting. She was trying to say something to him but it was too low to hear; the louder she became, the more he lost focus, and before long he blacked out.

When he woke up he was back in his room again, but this time he was not a ghost; he was now the emaciated patient inside the bed. He couldn't believe how real it felt this time. It was nothing like his former two visions, but he soon realized that it was now real. The blurry edge to his vision was no longer there and pain wracked his body from his toes to his head. Tricia didn't seem particularly excited that he was awake. She seemed aloof, as if him waking up to look around was nothing new to her.

"Trish, why am I here? How did I—what have you done to me?"

"Hello, Bradley," she said without looking at him.

"Trish! I've been looking all over for you. I thought I told you never to leave."

"So, is it to be Trish today, or would you like me to be Priscilla?"

What was she talking about? How could she be Priscilla? He thought. *Was the vision reality? The one where he was on the couch with Tricia?*

"How would you be Priscilla?"

"Brad, you haven't been well. Did you notice that I was gone for over a week while you sat out in your car talking to yourself? I have played along because I thought that in time you would be okay, but those pills you took, to buy me the skin to make me beautiful? They broke your mind."

"Broke my mind? No, I've been okay. I went to Miami to see Priscilla, and I drove back."

"You haven't left the apartment complex in over a year. You talked to yourself, you barely ate, and you spent most of the day sleeping and dreaming of a girl that doesn't exist."

He couldn't believe what he was hearing, but he tried to think back on the miserable drive that he had made from Miami and he could only remember the radio show. He had been exhausted during the drive, but it felt as if he had closed his eyes and woke up in the parking lot of his apartment complex. He was mad at Priscilla for the deceit, and the way she had treated him when he was there, but he was having trouble remembering faces. *What did Priscilla look like? Why was everything so hard to remember?*

"I'm... I'm just tired. I don't want to play these games with you. I've been driving for almost twenty hours and now I'm in bed with all of this... seriously, what is this?"

"May I see the correspondence you've had with this girl, Priscilla? If she is real, show me the records of her calling you or sending you a text message. Let's see it."

He picked up his device from the tray next to him and flipped through his text messages. The only thing he saw was an endless amount of missed calls from his mother. He looked into the calls and the emails. There was nothing of Priscilla—but he had already been through this.

"So, you've gone through my personal device and deleted all traces of Priscilla. I don't care. What I need to know is, what have you done to me?"

"I created something to help get the pills out of your system. You thought you had a girlfriend. What you had was an android, one that had enough intelligence to know that something was wrong, but not enough to realize she was being treated as two different women."

"But, that can't be so. Priscilla had her own place. We went out... there's no way that could have been you."

Tricia took Brad's hand and jabbed a needle into it. He flinched hard and yelled out loud, and she let his hand go so that he could rub at it. "What the hell was that for? I know I'm awake, okay."

"That feeling you have right now? It's called pain, and while we all dislike pain, it is one of the best indicators that we are indeed alive. When you built me you told me the same thing about pain and life, do you remember?"

"Not really. Did I hurt you?"

"For years you have been going about your life as if you weren't here. Let me ask you this. This Priscilla woman that you dated for so long. Have you been by her place?"

He looked at her, knowing she knew what he had found at Priscilla's place.

"There was no apartment, was there? Of course there wasn't; you barely left your home."

The tired feeling that took over his body became unbearable and before long he found that it was dark and he had woken up again. The constant drifting, and the similar yet different conversations he had with Tricia across varying dreams made him confused.

He saw her seated across the room, asleep. The android doctor was going through the motions of monitoring his vitals. He sat up and looked around. There were so many gaps in his memory, so many things he thought he'd experienced, but no details, as if they were imagined. Priscilla's face kept on changing, and the trip to Miami seemed to have happened so far in the past that he couldn't believe it.

Tricia said she had found a way to fix the effects of the pills. She had taken it upon herself to work on him, to re-wire his broken circuitry from the mystery drug that he—in his impulsive need to complete her construction—had voluntarily ingested. He felt proud of her, but frightened at the same time. He swung his legs off of the bed, removed the tubes, and tried to walk. It was at this time that he noticed his long toenails. Why had he not noticed how far his health had fallen? He remembered himself being healthy; he had felt strong enough to challenge the guy who ogled Priscilla at the basketball game. That couldn't have been more than a year ago. He remembered himself being healthy but the body he saw reflected in the mirror told a different story about his history.

He reached for his phone and called his mother. He needed to hear her voice more than anything else. He hadn't noticed the time, but it was 2 a.m., and his mother didn't answer the phone. He tried a few more times before his emotions took over and he began to weep loudly into his hands.

Tricia walked over and held him as he sobbed into her shoulder. "I'm sorry, Brad. I'm sorry for what you have gone through to make me."

"It doesn't matter. None of it matters. See, its life's bitter irony that makes me cry. I built you because I was lonely. I had nobody, but in doing this I lost everything that I did have, including my sanity and my intelligence. Now that I'm truly awake, I realize that I am a fool. You are all I have."

"I don't understand."

"The irony in this, Trish, is one that man has been guilty of since early times. We neglect the good that is in front of us in order to pursue what we cannot have. I built you to be my ultimate woman but then decided that I needed more; I needed a human. I could blame the pills. I mean, they did give me a false sense of confidence. But I started looking when I was sober and you were complete. I'm so stupid. Now look at me, a gross, walking skeleton with an imaginary girlfriend. No, even better than that, an imaginary girlfriend that doesn't want me."

Tricia helped him back to bed and re-attached his tubes before kissing him on the cheek and stroking his hair. "You will get better, but it will take some time for your body to take to the implants."

"Implants?"

"Your body is failing, and you won't live if I don't replace a few necessary parts. Don't worry about appearances, or how anyone else will see you. Your purpose is to innovate, and I will make sure you stay alive long enough to do just that. You will bring a new age to the field of robotics, and develop a race of androids that can assimilate into society and change the attitudes of the humans from within. How does that make you feel?"

"I like the sound of that, Tricia. I really do."

"See, everyone has a purpose, and my purpose was twofold. I was built to help my people, and I was meant to love you, and only you...unconditionally."

"THERE IS NOTHING MORE contradictory than the laws we have put in place for robotics. While we have always had contradictory, outdated laws, when will we say 'enough is enough' when it comes to the government being in our bedrooms? Time and time again we get heavy-handed laws passed because a section of this country allows themselves to be brainwashed by politicians and religious leaders that are on the politician's payroll."

"Come on now, Tom. You're going down a risky path now. How about you stick to the facts and not the suppositions and conspiracy theories that have always been the stomping ground of the poorly educated."

"Are you calling me poorly educated, sir?"

The two men on the discussion panel were fired up and ready to fight when the calm, elderly host reminded them they were on television and would do better to calm down and keep the discussion civil. She may as well have asked them to come up with a formula for time travel. One was android advocate, Dr. Thomas H. Lowell, and the other was a popular writer for a conservative magazine. Tricia had watched them going at it for the better part of an hour but she still couldn't understand the view of the conservative writer.

Thomas H. Lowell was a passionate man and some of his views were on the extreme side of crazy, but he was advocating for people's freedom more than androids. "A man or woman should be free to love who or what he wishes, as long as it doesn't hurt anyone." This was his message, and Tricia couldn't understand why everyone didn't agree with him. The writer had no real points; he seemed to only be on the show to quote from popular religious texts, and counter everything the doctor had to say. Still, it was entertaining and educational, and she stood in awe of the host's patience.

"For a long time there have been people marrying and loving dolls, pillows, holograms, imaginary people, you name it. No laws were passed to punish them for this. This persecution of people that happen to love androids is only in place because of fear and hate mongering, but more than anything else, it is because it is new."

"New? The last time I checked, doctor, perverts have always been a part of society AND they have always been punished by the law."

"Perverts? Is that what you call them, sir? Perverts. Do tell, what constitutes a pervert in your world of routines and appearances?"

"Just scan your device dictionary, Doc. You will find the definition of that word to be quite succinct. A pervert is someone with a lust for something that isn't considered ordinary. These androids, no matter how realistic they make them look, are not human beings. You cannot procreate with one, you cannot make them age, and if you don't restrain them, there is a good chance they will murder you in your sleep."

Dr. Lowell was furious. "Says who? When has there been an incident of murder by an android outside of gladiators, prostitutes, sports droids, and other glorified slaves that had suffered abuse by their masters? When has an unrestrained android been powered down for harming her master? I'll tell you when, never! So I think you need to watch your lies and accusations, especially when spreading your brand of propaganda all over the airwaves."

The two men made to fight again, but this time the host took them to commercial break while Tricia processed the discussion and what it meant for her future. There was a large segment of android supporters in Seattle, but there was also a large segment of people that would see them powered down and scrapped. They liked the world when androids were stiff, clunky machines that could perform only one duty. These droid killers had burned down factories, and had kidnapped droids one at a time to publicly burn them or melt them down. There was a time when Tricia had feared them, but Brad had helped her to become brave. The best weapon an android had against attackers was information, and this was why she watched as many shows on public opinion as she could.

"When it's your time, it's your time," Brad would say, and she had grown to believe it. If you could not help or predict the day that you no longer had life, why live in fear of it being tomorrow? She watched a lot of news now that Brad was in recovery and much of it had to do with change, the fear of change, and the vocal opponents of modern technology. It was the ugly part of the world that Brad could not show her, but the television stations were filled with it. Once she had become knowledgeable of the danger she was in just by being an android, she had searched for detailed information on it.

The first set of androids had come from Japan in the 21st century, but they were humanoid morons. They could perform one duty and it was restricted to the particular model. They could mow your lawn, paint your walls, and change out the wheels on a car in a pit stop, but they lacked intelligence, plasticine skin, and most importantly, the ability to expand. Their limbs were not as mobile as hers were now, and some rolled around on wheels, while others had to be carried. The ability to make a machine walk upright, maintain balance, and catch itself when falling did not come about for another twenty years.

There was a manufacturer that created a toy robot that was meant to play with children suffering from diseases that disallowed human contact. The project to develop this robot was backed by an agency that pulled in enough funding to help bolster the research and development. Patrick and Patricia the robot twins came about from their efforts. These robots could walk upright, run, pick themselves up, and most importantly, give gentle hugs. The twins revolutionized the robotics industry and when the company began to lose people due to a number of reasons, much of their secrets were leaked and before long all robots were walking, running, and moving more naturally. The adult movie industry saw this change and put their money behind a living sex doll that could be themed after women and men from their movies. Vanessa the sex-bot came from this, along with her male counterpart David. The models sold a lot of units and became a problem for many couples. Divorces increased, and this brought in the religious sect who made up rules against humans sleeping with machines.

The religious sect had always been a core driver for the thoughts of the people, so when these rules made their way into churches across the country, a number of hardcore groups were formed to reveal "perverts" that owned David and Vanessa dolls. Many people had their lives ruined when they got exposed for having one of these dolls, and there was pushback from others that felt strongly about people having sexual freedom. While this was going on the creators of household androids had upgraded their own models to look and act more human while performing their duties. The idea was that the more human an android looked, the less "strange" or "scary" they would seem. The evolution continued this way with technology getting better, and the religious trying to keep it from doing so.

Tricia was fascinated with her history, and she studied it day in and day out so that she knew every model's name, every manufacturer, and every key change that had moved things along. One part of the history that she found to be the most interesting was the underground community. If Brad was back in the older times with Vanessa and David dolls, he would have been a part of this community. They were programming intelligent machines, and like many of their projects throughout time, they made it competitive. They revealed their work to one another through videos on the internet. Some had made their Vanessa doll talk and enunciate words with her lips; others had found a way to introduce an adaptive A.I. so that she could remember likes and dislikes.

This competition went on for decades and before long the teenagers that were playing around with their parents sex-bots became the leaders of the industry, applying their knowledge to the commercial arena. Domestic androids became intelligent, walking mannequins in plasticine, and they could now do more duties to make human life easier. This, however made for more problems, but this time it was from the community. The number of jobs had decreased significantly, with companies buying androids to perform duties that a full time employee had to be paid for in the past. For large companies the androids were a godsend. They only needed to pay once to buy them, and while the cost was significant, the android represented an employee that would not get a salary, not ask for a raise, and didn't need any time off. The one time price compared to what it cost to maintain human labor was nothing, and before long it seemed like every job that did not require innovation and deep thought was being given to an android.

There were riots, burned down buildings, and violent protests over this change, and even more anti-android groups were formed to thin the herd of job-stealing machines being purchased. Android cab drivers went missing, protestors tore the heads off of any androids they came across, there were lawsuits, blackouts, refusal to purchase certain goods—you name it. This did not stop companies from using robot labor, and since it was a worldwide change, it only made sense for America to follow suit. What the government did to offset the new, jobless world was to implement new taxes on big companies, a change that came with a lot of its own fighting and political woes. The laws passed eventually, and the ridiculously rich company owners were forced to pay. People began to live easier, lazier lives, and the androids were literally everywhere.

One of the things that did not change much in terms of android/human relations was the taboo on relationships. To appease the strong religious sect that had started the revolution, the government made strict laws to dictate what could or could not be done with android technology. Androids were always to be easily identified as such—which was why synthetic skin that appeared human was outlawed. Androids were to stay restricted, and any sign of true artificial intelligence was to be reported. The reason for this was due to an angry engineer that had programmed his very human looking android to walk into a police station and set off an explosive. Now androids were not allowed to look "too human," could not freely walk the streets—unless it was part of their job—and couldn't be unrestrained.

Brad broke all of these laws when he developed Tricia, and she worried for him that she would be discovered. It was the reason that he kept her confined, and powered her down when he could. The only way that she could help him was to become more human in her actions. The history that she studied had revealed the ugliness that came with people when they saw an android. People disliked change, and they disliked different. America's history of occupation, racism, classism, sexism, and religious influence that aimed at persecuting anyone with a different look, sexual orientation, or belief, had not changed much by the time it came to acceptance of the working android.

She was an enemy in hostile territory, painted up to look like the ones that would do her harm. She would need to have the perfect speech, the perfect reactions, and the perfect story to avoid discovery. There were people out there that were actively looking for androids that had been built in violation of the laws, and if she was to be found out by one of them, Brad would be arrested for the rest of his life. It was exciting but scary at the same time, but she had been built to learn. So absorbing patterns, behavior, in order to become something else was a challenge that she was willing to accept.

www.ingramcontent.com/pod-product-compliance
Lightning Source LLC
Chambersburg PA
CBHW071303130626
46556CB00003B/1453